THE RANCHER TAKES HIS CONVENIENT BRIDE

THE RANGERS OF PURPLE HEART RANCH BOOK 1

SHANAE JOHNSON

Edited by Alyssa Breck

Manufactured in the United States of America
First Edition January 2020

Keaton could hear his heart pounding in his ears. Just like every time he was on the battlefield, the beats synced with the ticking of the second hand of a clock. A calm went over him in the face of the danger that awaited him. He inhaled, the oxygen adding fuel to the bravado that came naturally to him. He was a well-trained soldier, a superbly trained warrior. One of the best specimens of the 75th Ranger Regiment.

Stepping out of his hidey-hole where he'd taken cover after the first shots rang out, Keaton looked around. His sightline was clear, which did not bode well. His spidey senses tingled at the calm and quiet. War was a noisy, frenetic affair.

Something was wrong.

Keeping low to the ground, he poked his head out

to gather more intel. The camouflage of his clothes made it so that he blended with his environment. Even his gun was painted green and brown to mix in with the elements.

And then he heard it. A cry. A shot.

They sounded one after the other. Keaton's ears perked like a dog coming alert. Before storming into action, he deduced what he'd learned.

The cry had come from the left side. The shot had come from behind him. The blast from the gun had gone over his head. The cry from a human throat had come before the shot. There was no resulting thump of a body.

A tingle went up to his spine. Keaton rolled over onto his back just in time. A grizzly bear of a man was on him, weapon rising.

That's where the bear went wrong. A rising weapon was completely ineffective. Keaton's weapon was at the ready. His finger already on the trigger, which he squeezed.

The grizzly's body jerked from the direct hit. Pink paint-splattered exactly where his heart would lay if the traitor had one. Keaton fired off another and then another round.

"Hey," growled the grizzly man. "I'm down."

"You know you're on my team, right?" said Keaton.

Griffin "Grizz" Hayes grinned. His incisors glinted in the midday sun like a predator who knew he'd cornered his prey. Keaton knew that look. It was the same look Grizz had given him back in Basic Training when he decided to prank their drill sergeant.

Sergeant Cook never saw it coming. The sadistic sergeant never figured out who'd put Gorilla Glue on the inside of his hat. The entire squad had paid for that prank for months in extra drills in the middle of the night. But it had been worth it to stick it to that demon-born drill sergeant. The red marks of the glue had taken just as long to heal, reminding the soldiers of their revenge every day they ate mud and missed sleep.

So, why had Grizz turned on his best friend now? And why was he grinning after he'd been caught? The spidey tingles crawled over Keaton's skin again.

Keaton didn't remain glued to his spot. He hit the ground just as more shots rang out. Grizz let out a roar of laughter. So, it was a mutiny. His entire team was out to get him.

What for?

It couldn't be the late-night planning session Keaton held them in until well after one in the morning last Saturday. It couldn't be the fact that Keaton changed his mind twice, on which supplier to use, causing them to redo the books over again, and then again. It couldn't be the fact that he'd promised General Strauss that his team would have their Ranger Training Camp ready in just ninety days when the team had originally planned to take half a year to get things in gear, which didn't include any downtime after separating from the military.

The shots coming at him from all four directions told Keaton he was wrong. They'd divided into two equal teams, three on each. But the four remaining men all aimed their weapons at him.

Keaton was undaunted. As the leader of his team, he saw how he could use this mutiny as a teachable moment. A plan formed in his mind. He only had time to come up with two variables in case Plan A didn't work instead of his standard three. With the main plan and two backups, he moved into action.

Mac Kenzie's gaze connected with his. The recognition dawned in Mac's eyes. The two had been in many tough situations together. Enough that they could communicate without using words.

So Mac, or Mackenzie as everyone simply pushed his first and last name together, saw Keaton's entire plan in one glance. But again, Keaton was already locked and loaded a second before Mac rose to the occasion.

Keaton grabbed Mac by the shoulders. Rolling him over, Keaton sprang onto his feet, hefting all of Mac's six foot three, two-hundred-fifty-pound bulk of pure muscle.

"You son of a—" But Mac's words died as his body jerked, taking on pink and purple paint from the assault meant for Keaton.

Keaton swung his weapon up and under Mac's armpit. He took aim and fired, towing Jordan Spinelli and David Porco.

With two down, he had two more to go. He ducked around Grizz, plastering his front to the man's paint-smeared back. In a matter of seconds, Grizz's front matched his back. But not a speck got on Keaton.

From the protection of Grizz's massive bulk, Keaton opened fire on his last frenemy. Russell "Rusty" Hook, who was a perfect shot, went down immediately.

Keaton still didn't lower his weapon. "Surrender," he called out.

"Never," the five men said in unison. "Surrender is not a Ranger word." They all chuckled after reciting the end of the Ranger Creed.

Keaton lowered his weapon. He walked to Mac and helped the man up. Another part of the creed was that they never left a fallen comrade under any circumstances.

Keaton clapped Spinelli on his back and came away with pink and purple paint.

"Told you he had eyes in the back of his head," said Porco.

"Don't be ridiculous," said Keaton. "I have 360 vision. Like a hawk."

"You mean an owl," said Grizz. The man was the strong, silent type women always swooned over. He could often be found reading ancient poetry books.

But the weird part was that Grizz actually liked the riddle of words.

"Then I'm a super owl," Keaton countered. "Anyway, I think we can all learn something from this."

Five groans joined the chorus of chirping crickets and birdsong in the forest. Keaton thought he heard a paint gun safety click off.

"This was supposed to be a fun excursion in the midst of your insane work plan," said Mac.

"Don't knock the plan," said Keaton. "The plan is our ticket to not go to desk jobs."

After separating from service, many rangers went on to work in the intelligence community or in top-level security. But none of his guys wanted to work inside. They all craved the outdoors and the freedom to set their own schedules. There was still a lot of action in them. They just no longer had the desire to travel and dodge real bullets.

"The unexpected will happen to us as we move forward building the best training camp in these United States," said Keaton. "But, we'll always be ready to maneuver because we have a plan."

"Oh yeah?" said Rusty. "Maneuver this."

Keaton dodged the paint pellet. It caught him in the forearm, but it wasn't a direct hit.

Rusty rolled his eyes.

"Like a hawk," Keaton grinned.

"An owl," corrected Grizz.

Keaton shrugged.

"You sure about this location, though?" said Grizz. "The Purple Heart Ranch in Montana?"

"I've heard some crazy things happening up there," said Spinelli.

Keaton had heard them too. Soldiers going to heal the wounds they'd received in combat. Yet, in less than three months, each man had winded up in holy matrimony and no plans to leave the ranch. It was kind of like a cult. But Keaton knew the man in charge and knew him to be a top-notch soldier and a decent man.

Marriage wasn't a path Keaton planned to go down. He had a five-year plan before he even thought about marriage.

"We're not living on the land, so none of the rules or hoodoo will apply to us," he assured his men. "Our clients will stay six weeks, at the longest, which doesn't meet their three-month rule."

Apparently, the land of the Purple Heart Ranch had a zoning issue where if a soldier wanted to live on it, they had to be married within three months or hightail it out of there. It was backwoods, for sure. But they needed land in the backwoods to create their state-of-the-art course and facility.

"Good," said Grizz. "Cause myth or zoning, I have no plans for a wife."

There was a chorus of agreement. Except for Mac and Rusty. Mac had given a woman a ring, which she'd rejected more than once. Rusty had divorce papers sitting in his duffel bag. There was one signature on the ream of paperwork. It wasn't his signature.

"Let's get changed and head out," said Keaton. "We've got a lot of work to do and little time to do it. Living at the edge of a rehabilitation ranch and preparing for our first clients will keep us all too busy for dating."

"Whoa, whoa," said Porco, holding his hands up in surrender. "Put dating back in the plan. Those farm girls need a load of me in their lives."

Pops rang out as Porco was painted with a shower of bullets for that comment. With their ire turned away from himself, Keaton took a rare moment to relax and laugh at his brothers-in-arms and their antics.

His edict stood. With the amount of work they had to do in the next three months, none of them, himself especially, had time for dating. The training facility would be his sweetheart for the next five years before he even decided to look for a wife. That was the plan.

CHAPTER TWO

The sizzle of charred beef smelled different when said cow was alive and kicking and not quartered into pieces and placed in a pan. Brenda Vance backed up. She avoided the bull's hindquarters, but she wasn't quick enough to avoid the wood. The plank of the fencing splintered, and a shard of wood caught the side of her forehead.

Blood mixed with sweat and caught in her eye. Brenda swore. Her muttered curse made the younger three of her ranch hands wince. They should all wince. It was their fault the cow wasn't properly secure.

"You all right, missy?" came the gravely, tobacco tarnished voice of the fourth and eldest ranch hand. Manuel Bautista had stepped on this ranch around the time when Brenda had taken her first steps before she'd turned a year old. Like her, he knew this place inside and out. Unlike her, he was not the one in charge.

Brenda bit her tongue before she could utter another curse. Her brother might be a pastor, but she'd learned that his role didn't give her any extra free passes for the next life.

"Don't call me missy." She swiped the blood and sweat with her worn flannel shirt, getting a whiff of the hard work she put in this day. Looking up, she saw that two of the ranch hands' hands barely glistened in the hot afternoon sun. Their brand-new cowboy hats were starched perfect. Their shirts had not a single drop of sweat at the pits.

"It's Miss Vance," she said as she stared down at the blood on her shirt. "Or, boss."

As the elder ranch hand turned back to calm the new bull, Brenda caught the sound of a Spanish curse. Two of the other men chuckled. The skinny blond one in tight jeans that most certainly came from either Old Navy or Urban Outfitters was the one Brenda had nicknamed Yankee. The second chuckler, the one Brenda called Frat Boy, had a T-shirt with Greek letters stretched over his brown biceps. He'd claimed his great grandfather was one of the famed Buffalo soldiers. Though Brenda doubted that this kid came from that strong stock when he constantly swatted and yelped when any bug came near him, or any mark landed on any piece of his wardrobe.

The other hand didn't laugh. He pretended to look away. Not to be above it all. His attempt to not take a side was clear. His name Brenda knew. He was Angel Bautista, the nephew of her ornery elder ranch hand.

Angel was young, just out of high school. Born in a time where girls were told they could do or be anything, and they had examples and paths to follow. Angel's uncle had been born during a time when women's places were in the kitchen. Or, if she wanted to venture outside, in the garden.

The other two hands were outsiders. This was a semester internship for them. They'd be back to their city colleges in a couple of weeks' time. Whereas Angel lived here and would need to find and keep work on a ranch. He was stuck between two worlds with two elders to mind. Brenda wouldn't wait long to figure out who the kid would follow.

This was her life, her livelihood, and she needed good hands to keep it going. She'd been herding cattle just as long as she been riding horses. She'd been bruised feeding livestock. Broken a toe while changing out a horseshoe. A broken wrist while on a cattle run which she'd led on her own. You name it, she sprained it, strained, and might even have fractured it at some point in her line of work as the overseer on this ranch. And through it all, she'd never missed a day of work.

Brenda had done it on her own the last three years after her parents retired. But in those many years, she'd made the ranch so profitable that she'd grown the herd, thereby increasing the workload and the need for hands to help her.

With these sorry excuses for hands, she might as well be doing it on her own. Manuel refused to listen to her way of doing things, relying instead on the old ways. And the other men followed behind him, even though she was the one who signed their paychecks.

"Maybe you should head back inside the house," said Manuel. "To tend to your injury. It's dangerous work out here."

He left off the end of his sentence *for a woman*. At least he learned one lesson today.

This had all stemmed from her suggestion that they use sugar as well as grain to corral the new bull she'd just purchased so that they could brand it. Sugar would've helped calm the animal down. But it was a new way of doing things, and Manuel had balked. Then the bull had kicked out.

Brenda was too tired to fight. The blood still dripping in her eyes was making it hard to oversee what they were doing. She knew they weren't doing it the way she wanted them to do it. But the bull was branded, signifying that she was the owner. That was the major item on her to-do list for the day, so she might as well call it a day.

She banged through the back door of the big house and froze. The back door led directly into the house's kitchen. Dinner was sizzling in a pan. A perfectly cooked steak alongside roasted smashed potatoes just out of the oven and buttered green beans. The fridge was opened and a body hunched down inside. The door closed, and a man in an apron stood.

"You are truly a gift from God," said Brenda.

"And you're bleeding from the crown of your head," said the man. "But I don't see any thorns."

Brenda touched her hand to her forehead. The warm trickle of blood stained her fingertips. Luckily, there was no pain.

"If I go out there, am I going to find one of the ranch hands dead, Bren?"

Brenda sighed, disappointment clear on the gust of breath. "No, Walter. You won't be giving any last rites tonight."

Brenda's brother, Pastor Walter Vance, grabbed paper towels and pressed them to his sister's forehead.

"Ouch," she complained.

Walter ignored her. This wasn't the first time he'd cleaned her up after she'd broken skin. It had been a regular occurrence in the Vance household when they were kids. Might be one of the reasons he'd gone into the church. "Tell me what happened?"

"Incompetence. Chauvinism. Lazy ranch hands. That's what."

"I thought Bautista was one of the best?" said Walter.

"Maybe twenty years ago. The times have changed."

"Good thing that they have," said Walter. "With all the technology you've implemented into the ranch, you need fewer hands than when we were kids."

Their dad had left the ranch to both of them. But Walter gave up his share to Brenda and turned to the church. She was grateful. Especially since because her brother was not a partner, she didn't have to share with him just how much said new technology cost her, not to mention the new bull. She'd financed it, and the first payment was coming due. She didn't have enough cash liquid to keep up with all the bills and overhead.

"Bren, if something is wrong," her brother said, "you'd tell me?"

No, she wouldn't. "Of course, I would."

Brenda learned long ago that lying to a pastor didn't cause an immediate lightning strike. So, she had time. "As long as you keep coming over and cooking for me, all will be right with the world."

"Maybe you should marry," said Walter.

Brenda's utensils clattered down on the plate. This was one topic where her brother was not evolved. Brenda had no desire to get married. Men slowed her down. Case in point, her ranch hands were slowing her operation.

"You got a ranch full of soldiers next door," said Walter. "Some looking to marry in the next ninety days, as goes the regulations on the ranch land."

Which was why Brenda steered clear of her neighbors at the Purple Heart Ranch. And that included their boundary line, which forced individuals to get married just to stay on the healing ranch. She was sure the arrangement was illegal, yet no one had reported it.

"Didn't one of those soldiers run off with your fiancé?" she said.

Beth Cartwright, the pastor's daughter, had been engaged to Walter briefly. But then her childhood crush who had been MIA returned, sweeping her off her feet with a proposal and an engagement ring.

"Reese is a good man," said Walter. There was genuineness in his voice despite the bitterness of the breakup. "All of the soldiers are."

Walter was far too forgiving. But it was part of his job description. Brenda's job description was rancher. She didn't have time to be someone's wife. She was far too busy with cattle, more repair projects than she could fit on an 8 x 10 sheet of paper – single-spaced, and good for nothing ranch hands who she could see were headed to their trucks before sundown without getting their work done.

No. She was best left to her own devices. She doubted she would ever allow a man to take her hand.

CHAPTER THREE

Keaton looked at the passing scenery of the American heartland. The brown, majestic mountains with peeks of various colors. The rolling green pastures that seemed to stretch on into eternity. It surprised him how much this beautiful land mirrored the landscapes of Afghanistan, Iraq, and Syria. The only difference between the two landscapes was that hope and opportunity were in this fresh mountain air. War zones were rife with conflict, turmoil, and hopelessness.

During his service in each of those countries, Keaton had seen men die young. He'd witnessed as women and children suffered on a daily basis. He'd watched as the land was ravaged and torn apart by politics and projectiles.

Driving through the Main Street of this small

Montana town, the outlook was night and day. Looking out of the window of his rented red Jeep, Keaton saw children skipping down the streets. Moms trailed behind their youth in yoga pants paired with cowboy boots. A group of old men sat on neighboring porches smoking pipes and spitting tobacco. The earthy smell of baked bread permeated the air instead of the metallic aftertaste of explosive powders.

Keaton could see why the soldiers of the Purple Heart Ranch came here and chose to stay after their rehab. The landscape held the familiarity of where they'd been. But the people showcased the future of what they were all fighting for, a community where they belonged.

For the last six years, Keaton had returned to his hometown after each assignment. The hustle and bustle of the crowded city made him anxious. The tall gray buildings and cold concrete unsettled him. The blank stares of the people on the streets, their tight lips, even the eye rolls of strangers avoiding each other on the sidewalks, made Keaton prickle with worry.

Soldiers looked at each other in the eyes. They spoke plainly. They spoke clearly.

So, no, Keaton had not mixed well with civilian life. Neither had the other men when they'd each gone back home to their city lives. None of them wanted to actively engage in combat any longer. But they still wanted a piece of the action. In this place that looked like a war zone engulfed in peace, Keaton knew that each of them might be able to make a life.

Thirty minutes later, he pulled up to the gates of the Bellflower ranch. He knew he was in the right place when he saw the purple flower insignia on the iron bars. That lily-like flower was the symbol for wounded warriors. In patches of grass just off to the side of the paved path, Keaton saw more of the purple bellflowers. They were a native plant to this area. It looked as though they grew wild on this land. No wonder the wounded vets of this ranch felt at home here.

Driving through the gates and up the gravel path, Keaton saw the ranch was filled with soldiers in various states of healing. Men with prosthetic legs rode hard on horses. Weaving farther down the bend in the road, Keaton saw a garden where men with missing fingers and missing arms tilled the soil. Coming out of a barn were men with burns on their faces, arms, and legs. The soldiers tended to a menagerie of farm animals. Sheep and goats rubbed up against their scarred limbs as though unaware of any injury.

Keaton and his crew were fortunate that they'd return with all their limbs and faculties intact. Had any of them sustained any serious injuries, he knew this would be the best place for any soldier to come and heal. Furthermore, he hoped that any new soldiers aiming to improve their skills would come to the far side of the ranch, where he planned to build his elite training camp.

Keaton parked the Jeep at the big house where the road dead-ended. There were no numbers on any of the homes. The directions he'd been given told him to follow the road until it ended. Hopping out of the Jeep, Keaton saw the man he'd come here to meet.

Dylan Banks emerged from the double doors and marched forward. He was dressed in a denim shirt and khakis. One of his legs was tanned. The other was made of steel.

"Keaton, you made it."

"Good to see you again, Banks."

The two men clasped hands. Scarred palm met scarred palm. Rough fingers gripped and tugged inward. The old friends came in for a hug with many claps on the back. Keaton had served with Sgt. Dylan Banks on more than one mission. The man was sharp and could improvise in difficult situations with the best of them.

"Amazing set up you have here," said Keaton. "I've heard nothing but good things about this ranch."

"We take them all," said Banks. "The tired, the poor, the huddled masses."

"Isn't that the saying on the Statue of Liberty?" Keaton chuckled.

"Well, now we're taking in the wretched refuse like Army Rangers."

Banks struck out an arm, aiming a fist at Keaton. Keaton saw the move coming and held still to receive it. It was all in good fun.

"Ah, is Banksy-wanksy still upset that he couldn't pass the Ranger PFT?"

"Shut it," said Banks, but there was no bite to his bark. "I only missed it by a couple of points. It was the water survival section that drowned me."

"You're from an island."

"I'm from New York City."

Keaton shrugged. The qualifications to become one of the elite Army Rangers were not a joke or a drill. Every month over four hundred eager souls arrived at Fort Benning, Georgia with the hopes that they might have the right stuff to accomplish the challenge. Fifty-one percent went home with their hopes dashed in the mud. The only reason Keaton had survived the training was that he'd prepared for the physical tests like a maniac.

That was what he planned to do with the training camp; train others the way he'd trained to pass the test. Boots On the Ground Elite Training was a dream Keaton didn't realize he had until he faced the nightmare that was the United States Army Ranger school. He knew he could never prepare any soldier fully for that experience. But anyone who passed through his training regimen had a better shot to be in the better half of that percentile.

"By next year, you'll be up and running," said Banks.

"Next year?" Keaton scoffed. "The plan is to open the doors in ninety days."

Banks scratched at the stubble of his jaw as he regarded Keaton. The incredulous look in his eyes said it all.

"It's ambitious," said Keaton. "I know. But I have a well thought out plan that will work if executed properly."

"Of course, you do," Banks chuckled, clapping Keaton on the back again. "I believe you can do it. Amazing things can happen in ninety days, especially on this ranch."

Now it was Keaton's turn to scratch at the stubble on his chin. He knew what that reference meant. Many of the men who came here to heal wound up getting married in that time period. Rumor had it, it wasn't just the zoning laws that governed occupancy on the ranch. Many believed it was something about the land itself.

Keaton was not a superstitious man. Even with that, he had no plans to live on the land. He only needed to work on it. So, the rules and the myths would have no bearing on him nor his business.

"Let's go take a look at the parcel your leasing," said Banks.

They hopped into a golf cart and took off. If Keaton thought the land was beautiful from afar, it was breathtaking up close. Colors kept switching from green pastures, to fertile brown dirt, to a rainbow riot of blooms. Interspersed were horses of brown, white, and black. Sheep with fluffy poofs of hair ... and an array of the rangiest mutts he'd ever seen.

Five dogs barked as they drove by. A few of them had a prosthetic attachment. One even had a wheelchair attached to his hind legs.

"Those are mine," said Dylan. "Well, they're my wife's. But they came with her in the marriage, so ..."

Keaton didn't bother to question the strangeness of this place any further. He kept his gaze trained on the land, making mental notes of how his clients would access the training facilities. At the edge of the ranch, Keaton saw his vision come to life. There, in the untouched land, was where he would carve out a dry patch from a mud pit where his students would learn the joy of crab walking, push-ups, and sit-ups.

Instead of buying lumber, they could chop down a couple of those trees to the right and make a climbing wall. The main thing they had to build was the indoor training facility and bunks. That and the specialty training area, which would take advantage of the mix of terrains from dry earth, to green pasture, to rocky hills, and the creek. That's where they'd put in installations to train special forces for covert missions.

"Can you pull up closer to the creek?" asked Keaton.

Instead of pulling closer, Banks slowed the vehicle. "The creek isn't within our boundaries."

It took Keaton a moment before the words made sense. When they did, his heart sank. He needed that creek for the special forces area. Heck, he needed it as part of the Ranger PFT training. Banks surely had to know that.

"It's owned by the neighboring ranch," said Banks.

"Do you think he'd be willing to sell or lease it for our purposes?" Keaton asked.

Dylan pursed his lips. "Not sure if *she* would. But you can go over and ask her. She's reasonable. Most days."

CHAPTER FOUR

Brenda didn't have an alarm clock in her bedroom. It was the smell of the coffee brewing that woke her. She'd brought herself one of those fancy coffee makers with a timer that magically poured her a cup each morning before the sun came up. Best purchase of her life.

She let the aroma lead her down the stairs like they were fingers in her nose, pulling her along. She was surprised her feet didn't come up off the ground as she made her way to the kitchen and the automatic coffee maker. Pulling two mugs from the cabinet, Brenda poured herself two cups. Like every day of her adult life, she would drink the first one down, letting the hot water burn her tongue and wake up all her brain cells. By the time she finished the first, the second one would be room temperature and ready to savor.

She reached in the fridge for the milk. Only to put the pitcher back. She'd grabbed for the milk that had come straight from the cow instead of the skim milk.

Finally, with her double dose of caffeine in her veins, Brenda ran a brush through her hair. She lost the battle with the tangles, so she gathered her tresses into a ponytail. She pulled a clean shirt over her head and jeans up her legs. Stepping into her boots, she was out the door before the first rays of the new day sun poked over the horizon.

She pulled the notepad from the back of her pocket. Flipping open the pad, she surveyed her list. Most of her chores were the same every day. There was always bale to stack, bale to move, feed to grind, manure to haul, bills to pay, and a fence to fix.

The only fence she was worried over today was the fencing that kept her new prize bull in. She knew the beast was raring to get his job done. But that would have to wait. She had to wean the calves from their mothers and set the newly independent beasts out in their own pasture.

The rooster stretched his feathers as Brenda walked past the coop. He was a slacker like the rest of her ranch hands. None of which were there yet.

Instead of growling about it, Brenda got down to work. She had half her chores checked off her list before the sun blinked a ray open at the horizon.

Brenda climbed on the tractor. It was an older

model, older than her. But it worked just fine. She jammed in the specialized key, better known as a screwdriver. The actual key had been lost months ago, somewhere out in her vast acreage. The engine turned over immediately, and she got to work.

By the time she'd worked the land and brought the tractor back, her ranch hands had finally shown up. Late. Again.

Just because she was a woman, they thought they could take advantage of her. Also, because it was late in the season, and most ranch hands had already been hired. She'd gotten the scraps of workers. Manuel was a holdover from her grandfather's time. His nephew was a good worker when he was away from his uncle's gnarled guidance. The other two were pretty much useless outside of being able to lift heavy things. She'd done more this morning than all four of them combined had done all week.

Brenda put the tractor in park. She remembered the specialized key and put it to work at its third job of the day. Twisting her ponytail into a bun, she jammed the screwdriver into her tresses. To keep her hair out of her face. And off her shoulders. And, yes, potentially as a weapon for what she had to do.

"You're late," she said. "Again."

Manuel grinned. "Sorry, honey. But the cattle don't know the difference."

Brenda clenched her fists. But she didn't reach for

the screwdriver. Yet. Though she was having very happy visions imagining Manuel's head as an ignition that needed help getting started. Actually, that wasn't far from the truth. The man was stuck in the dark ages of ranching. He needed a jumpstart. But Brenda was sure it was too late for him.

"I'm not your honey," she said calmly. "I'm your boss. But it doesn't look like I'll be that much longer."

"Don't tell me." Manuel's bushy brows lifted. His crooked grin rearranged his wrinkled face into something distasteful. "You're finally getting yourself a husband?"

The three younger men winced. No surprise there. All three of them were born into this generation, where they'd seen women wield power and respect. Manuel was about to get a time and culture shock.

"Let me be clear," said Brenda. "Your services are no longer needed here on the ranch."

Manuel's face contorted into something ugly. It reminded Brenda of the bull receiving his brand. The hiss of pain. The shock of betrayal. The shudder of resignation.

Brenda braced for Manuel to lash out. But he held still. It was the three men behind him that fidgeted like nervous newborn foals.

"You firing me, missy?"

"Good." Brenda stretched her lips into a cruel grin to match his. "I don't have to use smaller words."

His shoulders snapped straight. His fists curled. His mustache twitched. Dark shadows moved across his face as he dipped his head low so that his hat shielded his gaze.

Brenda held her ground. This was her ranch. It was her livelihood on the line. They all could go and find other work, with a man whom they might respect.

Or not. She didn't care. All she cared about was the running of and respect for her ranch.

"Now see here, Miss Vance."

Yeah! He had finally used the word *miss* appropriately. If she had a gold star, she still wouldn't give it to him. Too little, too late. He'd failed. And he was getting expelled.

"Without us, you have no hope of keeping this ranch up and running. It's calving season. It's not a one-man job. Definitely not a job for a woman."

The multitude of checkmarks on the list in her back pocket would beg to differ. But he was right. She couldn't do it all on her own. She would need a hand. Just not his.

She might've trained the younger three. But with the gnarled hand of Manuel having brainwashed them, they were as useless to her as a castrated bull.

"It is no longer your concern," she said.

Manuel curled his lip. His mustached twitched, making him look like the villain in some cartoon. Part of Brenda wanted to laugh. Instead, she looked behind him to see if she might salvage anything.

"If any of you lot are interested in staying, I'm willing to consider retraining."

There was a spark in each of their eyes. Well, the two city boys' eyes. Angel looked away, hiding his feelings on the matter from his uncle and Brenda alike. But Brenda took that as answer enough.

"They won't be led by your apron strings," said Manuel. "You won't make it a week without us. Let's go, boys. We get a weeklong break before she comes crawling back."

The two city boys looked at each other. Then they shuffled back to Manuel's truck. From the corner of her eye, Brenda caught Angel's wince. But he fell in line and trudged back to the truck as well.

"There are no hands available at this time in the season," Manuel said to her. "Can't wait to see you on your knees when you come begging for help."

"Why don't you hold your breath waiting for that to happen," she said.

With a youthful grace that belied his wrinkles, Manuel hopped into the driver's seat and took off. Brenda was about to let out a sigh of relief. She also let the floodgates of worry and anxiety about what she would do open. He was right. Help would be hard to find at this point in the season.

And then the truck stopped. Brenda used her hand

to shield her eyes as she peered at the back of the truck. It was halfway to the gate to her property.

Had they come to their senses? Did they want to come back and play by her rules? Would she allow it?

Before she could answer any of those internal questions, Manuel hopped out. He lifted his booted foot and kicked at a weak spot in the fencing. It was the bullpen. The pen that housed her new, pricey bull.

Manuel tipped his hat, hopped back in, and peeled out of her ranch.

The bull was at the center of the pen, and his back was turned. Brenda knew that she wasn't going to make it in time before he escaped. But she had to try. Any damage he might cause, she would be liable for, and she couldn't afford it.

She moved quick. Grabbing a sack of grain with one hand and a bag of sugar with the other, she hopped back on the tractor. She pulled the key from her hair and jammed it into the ignition.

The tractor stalled. She tried again. The bull had turned and was walking gingerly toward the broken fence.

Finally, the engine turned over. Brenda took off. But at twenty miles per hour, she was already too late. Her only hope was to corral the bull before he could hurt himself or anyone else.

Off in the distance, she saw a Jeep turn into her

gates. A red Jeep. A red Jeep headed straight toward her bull.

Who drove a red Jeep on a cattle ranch? Of course, Brenda knew that bulls were color blind. But it was a superstition nonetheless.

Brenda gunned the tractor, topping twenty-five miles per hour. She was too late. The bull spotted the red Jeep and rammed into it.

CHAPTER FIVE

Keaton had taken many hits in his lifetime. He'd studied Brazilian Jiu Jitsu where he'd been lifted and thrown bodily across a five-point ring. He'd been kicked in the chest during hand to hand combat training. He'd even had a round hit him in his body armor.

Each hit had rattled him. Each impact had made his vision go blurry. Had made his thoughts scatter, but never too far. Each time, he'd quickly regained his equilibrium and was back in fighting form within a few seconds, a moment at the max.

The great beast barreling toward him was bigger than the pro wrestlers and martial artists he'd faced in the ring. Its hooves tore up the ground each time its feet kicked against the earth to push it faster toward Keaton. Both vehicle and bull were going at the same speed, though the bull may have had a couple of miles on Keaton's Jeep.

In any case, Keaton was not going to outrun this fate. He did the only thing he could. He braced for impact.

Which was a mistake. Tense muscles and tense bones were more prone to injury than relaxed ones. But there was no way he was about to relax. There was an eight-hundred-pound bull headed straight for his driver's side door.

The metal door was no comparison to the armor plate inside a bulletproof vest. Car manufacturers had yet to make a bull proof, well, anything. Metal crunched as the door bent to the bull's will.

Keaton felt the impact on his shoulder and right side. But it was the booming crash that rattled him. The sound ripped his sense of equilibrium in half. He felt that the rug that had been pulled out from under him was the rug on the floor of the entire world.

The bull clearly felt the effects, too. It stood outside the door of the Jeep. Stunned. Its eyes were unblinking. Its breathing slow and ragged. For all the damage it caused the jeep, Keaton was sure the bull had to be bleeding internally.

A dust trail in the distance caught his attention. A tractor was coming toward him. Behind the wheel sat what he could only describe as an Amazonian warrior.

Long, brown hair flew behind her. Her toned arms

had the type of muscles a woman got from a hard day's work and not in choreographed kicks and twists at the gym. Her lips were pursed with concentration. Her gaze was focused. Keaton felt the urge to know what the color that determined gaze was.

Instinctively, his hand reached for the door to let him out of the Jeep. He pushed, but the door only went a couple of inches. Not enough for him to scoot his body out.

"Stay put," the warrior woman shouted.

There was so much command in her voice that Keaton did as he was told. The avenging angel put the tractor in park. She leaped out the door before the wheels came to a full stop. Her motion slowed, and it was as though he was watching one of those action movies with the slowed-down fast motion.

No. It wasn't her motion that was slow. It had to be his brain.

He knew she moved quickly, efficiently. But his eyes seemed to want to linger on her motions. Each action she took, his brain set up the replay, like in a football game when a play had to be reviewed.

Her hands raised slowly. Her voice was soothing, calming. Her words were pretty but unintelligible. But their meaning was clear.

Relax.

Everything's okay.

Come with me.

I'll make it better.

Keaton's whole being relaxed. All the pain from the impact dissipated. He was absolutely going to come with this woman who promised to make him better. He felt like a better man just being in her presence.

He tried to open the car door again. Again, it barely budged. Time returned to normal speed, and he caught a flash. It was his warrior angel. She'd flashed her eyes up at him.

They were green, by the way. Green like a blade of grass. A sharp blade of grass that just might leave a nasty cut. So, why did he have the urge to roll around in the pastures of her gaze?

"It's okay, big guy," she said.

Her voice had a dulcet quality. But it was soft as if the feathers were made of steel. It made Keaton's spidey senses tingle. Not over his skin like a premonition of danger. This sensation went straight into his bloodstream like it was a shot of adrenaline. Again, he tried to make his way out of the Jeep and to her.

"I've got this, soldier," she said.

"Let me help," he said.

"You're not part of the plan."

Keaton frowned at that. A plan that he was not a part of? It did not compute. He added a new item to his to-do list; get on board with this warrior angel's plan. Whatever it may be.

Her plan looked like she was going to corral the stunned bull back through the gaping hole in the fence. With a bag of grain and white granules that looked like salt, or maybe sugar.

The bull shook its head as though it was waking from a dream. It blinked a couple of times and then focused on her. Its nostrils puffed out gusts of air.

Was it going to ram her? It had already run into Keaton. He knew at that moment that he would die before he let anything hurt this woman. Whatever her original plan, Keaton was instituting Plan B.

He shoved out of the vehicle. Only for his back to hit the Jeep's door at her annoyed demand that he stay put. He ignored that. His boots hit the ground.

Followed by his knees.

And then his shoulders.

And, finally, his head.

The last thing Keaton realized before he passed out was that the white granules she'd tossed at the bull weren't salt. They were sugar. He wondered if he kissed her pouting, disapproving lips if she would taste as sweet?

CHAPTER SIX

"I was able to stop the internal bleeding." Maggie Banks gathered her tools and began placing them back in her veterinarian's bag. "He's going to take a while to heal, which means he's definitely going to be out of commission for the breeding season."

Brenda pressed both her thumbs to her temples. The other four fingers she raised to the Heavens as though in prayer. For guidance? For patience? For a miracle? Probably all three.

As if her short handedness wasn't enough. Now, her prized bull, which she'd sunk most of her liquid cash in, was useless. How was she going to make more babies to replace the cows she would have to separate from the herd and sell? And find the help to do it?

Manuel was right. With the size of her herd, this was not a one-man job.

Letting out a moan, Brenda dropped her hands. Her voice was rough and deep. It appeared to have gotten deeper with the hole she was now in. No, that sound hadn't come from her. It had come from the soldier whose jeep had been the unlucky matador's cape in this debacle.

Brenda had propped him up in the shade against the fence. She was a strong woman, but he had been far too heavy to lug inside. He was a big guy, but definitely not out of shape. He had thick legs made for horseback riding, though he clearly hadn't been near a horse lately if a Jeep was his mode of transportation in cattle country and farmland. His arms were the type that could wrap around a barrel and lift it. But she bet he'd likely been using those guns to carry, well, guns. His shirt had come untucked when he'd collapsed, and Brenda had been treated to a view of his six-pack.

Suddenly, she was thirsty for a beer to cool down. From all the exertion. Of corralling the bull.

Her cheeks were obviously flushed because of her anger at her former ranch hands. Still, the cold beer sounded good. But that would have to wait until after her bull was tended to.

"Can I check on *him* now?" asked Maggie.

Maggie had tried to tend to the soldier first, him being a human and all. Brenda had waited impatiently, insisting the man was still breathing, and that was the best they could do. Now that her bull was stable, she gave a head nod, acquiescing that Maggie could turn her attention to the man.

"Sergeant Keaton?" said Maggie.

The man blinked, opening groggy eyes. Cloudy like the sky after a storm. That was Brenda's favorite time; after the rain had washed away all the dirt and dust and left behind a fresh slate. After a storm was the time when things could begin anew. A fresh start. Because the worst had been done.

Sergeant Keaton fixed his clear-eyed gaze on Brenda. There wasn't any hint of cloud. In his eyes, Brenda saw the perfect fresh start.

Brenda felt corralled by his look like her entire body would go wherever he directed. Which was nuts. It had to be that weird Purple Heart Ranch hoodoo. He and Maggie must have brought it onto her land. Well, they'd be getting up and getting off her land soon. She had no need of a husband.

"How many fingers am I holding up?" asked Maggie.

Sergeant Keaton blinked, turning his clear eyes away from Brenda. His gaze went hazy as he looked at Maggie's two fingers. He canted his head, leaning away to peer around Maggie's hand at Brenda.

"Are you okay?" he asked.

Was she okay? He was the one that casually

bumped into an eight-hundred-pound bull. And he was asking about her.

"It didn't get you, did it?" he asked.

"The bull?" said Brenda. "No. He got you. And your Jeep."

Brenda's thumbs went back to her temples. Her fingers straightened back up to Heaven. But she knew no miracle was forthcoming to take care of the damage her bull had done to that car. Legally, she was responsible. Even though it was Manuel's maliciousness. Unfortunately, that argument wouldn't hold up in court.

Her land. Her bull. Her responsibility.

"Look," she said, dropping her thumbs when the throbbing continued all around the crown of her head. "I'll file an insurance claim for your vehicle and cover your medical bills."

It would set her back even more. But it was the law. It was also the right thing to do. And her parents had raised her to do right.

"I'm fine," said Sergeant Keaton.

He shifted his big body, trying to get his feet under him. As he leaned forward, Brenda got a clear sight of a strong chest with a dusting of fine hair. Even though his pectorals looked like they were solid as a rock, she was willing to bet that they'd be soft as pillows if she were to rest her weary head upon them.

"Brenda," grunted Maggie, "a little help?"

"Hunh?" Brenda blinked. "Oh. Right."

Maggie had grabbed one side of the soldier. Brenda rushed to his other side. Instead of focusing on righting himself, he grinned down at Brenda.

"You're strong," he said.

"You're weak," she said.

"Am not." He frowned. "I can do fifty-eight pushups, sixty-nine sit-ups, and run five miles in a half-hour."

"Those are the requirements to pass the Army Ranger exam," said Maggie.

"It's not an exam," said Sergeant Keaton. "It's a test of physical fitness, which you can't pass if you're weak."

"Well," said Brenda. "I bet those are great in the army. But they mean nothing on a ranch."

"Can you complete a twelve-mile march with a thirty-five-pound pack on your back?"

"No, but I can drive a herd of cattle ten miles with nothing but a length of rope and a sidearm."

They stood toe to toe now. Sergeant Keaton had a head over Brenda. Brenda was tall. She wasn't used to guys being on her level. Definitely not above it. Despite her attempts to knock him down a peg, she had the feeling she'd met her match.

"Sergeant Keaton," said Maggie. "You should take it easy. You were just in an accident."

"I promise I'm fine." He didn't take his eyes off

Brenda as he made the assertion. "No need to file any forms. The car is insured. I got the accident plan."

He did? The one that rental car companies tried to scare customers into purchasing before they handed over the keys even though it was unlikely they'd ever need it? Brenda got the feeling a man like Sergeant Keaton wouldn't fall for that. She had the suspicion that he'd bought the accident insurance on purpose.

Who does that?

"I feel fine," he continued. "But, I'll get checked out by the doctors at the Purple Heart Ranch if it'll stop you two from glaring at me."

Well, that was a load off of Brenda's checkbook. She'd take him up on it. Now, she had two fewer bills to pay. But that didn't answer the question that had been nagging her since she'd seen his Jeep in the distance.

"What are you doing here?" she asked. "Did you get lost?"

"No," he said, testing his balance by stretching those bulging arm muscles. "This is where I'm meant to be."

Something about that statement sent a tingle down her spine. It had the ring of truth to it.

"Meant to be what?" she asked.

"I was looking for you."

"Me?"

"I need something from you."

"From me?" Her voice sounded breathy to her own

ears. Brenda was never breathy. And definitely not for some guy. But her breathing was shallow as she hung on his every word.

"I need your land," he said.

The air slapped into her lungs from the gasp. The quick inflation made her head light. All the warmth went cold.

"Just the edge of it," he went on. "Where the creek is. I'll pay its value if I can get it by the end of the week."

The creek? At value? That would be enough to secure her debts, buy another bull, and maybe even hire a decent ranch hand or two.

"You got yourself a deal," said Brenda.

She stuck out her hand. Sergeant Keaton took it gingerly. When his fingers closed around hers, she felt a zing. The force was like the kick from a bull. By the look on his face, she knew he felt it too.

But they'd both been taken down by the same bull.

That was all it was.

CHAPTER SEVEN

"The deal is a no go."

Keaton sat in State Senator, Ginger Chase's office. The pretty blonde stared at her computer screen. Her fingers flew on the keyboard as though she were chasing after the insurgent that was standing in their way. But Keaton's attention was on the beautiful brunette next to him.

Brenda Vance had changed out of her jeans and T-shirt and into a nicer pair of jeans and a blouse. The new jeans were a darker blue and played perfectly against her tanned skin. The blouse, which was buttoned all the way up, still showcased the line of her neck, making Keaton's mouth thirst.

She'd driven them into town in her old Ford F150. The AC had worked, so she'd rolled the windows up and put the radio on. It had been for the best. Keaton was at a loss as to what to say to the woman. Brenda seemed perfectly content with the silence between them. So, he'd closed his eyes and let her take the wheel.

Keaton's rental car company had arrived and towed the ruined Jeep back into town. The owner hadn't been happy when he remembered that Keaton had taken out the insurance policy. Of course, he'd taken out the insurance policy. What responsible adult wouldn't?

Since the rental car company was on the same street alongside the city council building, he and Brenda had decided to kill two birds with one stone and stopped in. No appointment was necessary, as Maggie Banks had called ahead. Ginger was family, she'd said. However, Keaton didn't see any physical resemblance.

"I swear with the backward ordinances in this town, it's a wonder anyone stays here." Ginger's husband, Sergeant Colin Chase, leaned over his wife's chair.

Ginger turned her face up to his. "It kept you here."

"You kept me here," Chase countered.

Keaton looked away as the newlyweds made otter eyes at each other. Chase had come with his team to the Purple Heart Ranch nearly a year ago to find healing and rehabilitation after a mission gone wrong. Now, each of the four-man Fire Team was living on or near the ranch in wedded bliss.

The happiness and love between the two were palpable. It was nice; having someone who you could both depend on, and then go on and kiss. A soft place to fall at the end of a hard mission. Keaton wondered if maybe he'd move his five-year plan up a year or two. Maybe he could make time for dating even sooner.

His gaze latched onto Brenda as she leaned forward in the seat beside him. Her lips twisted in impatience as she cleared her throat. It took a second, and a louder throat clearing, for the lip-locked married couple to focus on the matter at hand.

"You're saying I can't sell my land to a willing buyer because of some ordinance?" asked Brenda.

"No, you can," said Ginger. "Just not as quickly as you'd like. The sale will take six months to go through. And in that time, no new construction can take place by anyone but the owner."

That caught Keaton's attention and broke his study of Brenda Vance's lips. "I need to be up and running in ninety days. My guys will be here tomorrow. We need to break ground by the end of the week to stay on schedule."

He'd planned for some setbacks. But not any of this magnitude. Six months? They couldn't afford to wait around for six months. They'd lose all their contracts, the contracts that would set the business into the black. He hadn't gone to the government to gain land for this very reason. The bureaucratic red tape took time to unravel. But here it was rearing its sticky head.

"There has to be a way around this," said Keaton, his brain already going into tactical overdrive, trying to suss out a workaround.

"Well," said Chase. "There is one way that I can think of."

Both Brenda and Keaton leaned forward eagerly. Before Chase responded, he glanced at his wife. The two shared a knowing look. It was the same silent communication Keaton had with Grizz when they were about to slip into some hairy business on the battlefield. Except there was adoration in this couple's look. Not an any-last-words kinda look he'd often exchanged with his best friend.

Keaton had never had a connection like that with a woman. One where words weren't needed. He'd learned communication was key with the fairer sex. But at the same time, women didn't like blunt honesty.

Whatever nonverbal words transpired between Ginger and Chase, they clearly understood each other perfectly and were on the same page.

Another glance at Brenda and Keaton got the impression she'd clued in on this silent exchange. Her expression changed from eager interest to total denial. She was also no longer leaning forward. She had pressed her body back into the chair, as though she was trying to get as far away as possible from the couple and their impending words.

What was going on?

"If you two are thinking what I think you're thinking ..." Brenda waved her finger at them. Then she waved both hands, as though warding them off. Then she huffed and crossed her arms over her chest in the universal language of back off. "Then, don't even."

Ginger and Chase only smiled. From the little he knew of Brenda Vance, Keaton knew she wasn't a woman who rattled easily. She'd faced down a bull with only a bag of grain and sugar. But looking at her in the chair, she looked completely rattled.

"What's going on?" Keaton asked the question to Brenda. He wondered if he'd get the message looking into her eyes. But she wouldn't meet his gaze.

"There has to be another way," said Brenda.

"We could get the law changed," said Ginger. "But that would take even longer."

"What if I leased the land to him instead of selling it?" asked Brenda.

"That could work, but it would still take time. Less time. Maybe two to three months before any construction could start."

"Neither of those options work for me," said Keaton. "We have a client booked for ninety days from now. They'll put us in the black for the whole year. We have to be ready, or we'll lose the contract."

He looked around the room. Ginger looked sympathetic. Chase looked amused. Brenda looked furious.

"What's this other way you're not telling me about?" Keaton said.

Keaton directed his comment to Chase. Chase looked to his wife. Ginger looked at Brenda. Brenda threw up her hands and faced Keaton.

"They're suggesting we get married," said Brenda.

Indignation rang through her voice. Her fingers flicked at the air like she was brushing the ridiculous notion aside. The corners of her eyes crinkled, and her brow creased as though the idea was insane.

But Keaton's brain was working, adjusting his master plan. Suddenly, the notion of waiting five years to find the perfect woman didn't seem so necessary. It wasn't ridiculous that he could squeeze Brenda into the plan. He could shift some things around.

Which was insane. Right? It had to be the bump on his head from the bull. Right? Even though the idea made his head stop hurting and his heart race.

CHAPTER EIGHT

"This town is absolutely insane." Brenda glared at the flashing red Don't Walk light. She tapped her foot impatiently as the light counted down. Counting was not going to calm her down. She needed to find a green light to get this moving.

"Yeah," Keaton sighed.

He stood beside her on the street corner. He'd had nothing but monosyllabic answers since they'd stormed out of Ginger's office. Well, she had stormed. He'd followed her, walking quietly in his combat boots. Too bad. Brenda was sure they'd sound like thunder rolling in if he was stomping mad.

Why wasn't he stomping mad?

His plans were being thwarted by bureaucratic red tape that should not hold up in a court of law. He clearly wasn't from this part of the country. Even though his muscles looked like they were crafted for bull wrangling.

But the way he carried himself, the straightness of his spine told her he spent more time in taxicabs and Ubers than crouched over a fast running horse. The way his grin held just a little back, as though he hadn't known his neighbors all his life, or maybe he hadn't met each of the people that lived around him. That told her that there stood a city boy through and through.

The light changed to green. Before she stepped into the street, Keaton crossed behind her. His fingers ghosted her low back. Not touching. But close enough that she could feel their impression. Once he was on the side of the street closest to the waiting cars, he fell back into step with her.

He had country manners. A man should always place his body between traffic and a woman. It was a ridiculous notion because if a car jumped the curb, it was barreling into both of them. But the thought was nice.

"Sometimes, I hate this town," said Brenda. "At every turn, someone is insisting you get married. Be it in church, on the Purple Heart Ranch, or at the kitchen table."

If it wasn't her former ranch hand, then it was her

brother. If it wasn't her brother, then it was the city government.

"I see," said Keaton.

Two words this time. So, progress.

Keaton shoved his hands in his pockets and hunched his shoulders. He hadn't looked at her since leaving Ginger Chase's office. They still didn't have a viable solution to this mess.

Clearly, marriage was out of the question. It wasn't even a question. The people in this town needed to stop trying to solve business issues with matrimony. It wasn't that easy.

"What if it was that easy?" said Keaton, coming to a stop.

"What if what were that easy?" Brenda asked as she turned to face him.

Keaton's gaze was fixed upon the building in front of them. They were standing at the City Hall. The building was a two-story affair. The mayor and his staff occupied the top floor. On the ground floor was where most civic matters were taken care of. Things like filing lawsuits, paying for violations, and getting marriage licenses.

Brenda's gaze jerked from the building and back to the man standing toe to toe with her.

"What if we did it?" he said.

"Did what?" She couldn't voice it. She could barely

even think it. But her mind was already getting away from her.

"What if we got married?"

"Maybe we should stop by the ER," said Brenda. "That was a pretty bad hit you took."

Keaton only grinned. It was a full grin, the kind she was sure he'd give to someone he'd known a lifetime. Why was he giving it to her when he hadn't known her for a day?

It was a dangerous grin. A grin she wouldn't mind seeing for a lifetime. Every self-preserving bone in Brenda's body told her to take a step back from him. Brenda held perfectly still under the assault of that heart-stopping grin.

"I'm fine," Keaton said. "I'm thinking clearly. I'm thinking logically."

He ran a hand through his hair. It wasn't exactly a buzz cut. Which meant he'd been out of the service long enough to let it grow. Brenda wondered what his hair would look like if the locks touched his ears. She wondered what it would feel like if her fingertips brushed the wayward strand of hair that fell onto his forehead.

"Is there really much difference between a marriage contract and a leasing agreement?" he asked. "In a sense, it's all about ownership."

"But in marriage, you would own my property and me."

Something flashed in his gaze. Like a predator flashing his pupils in the dark at helpless prey. Brenda wasn't easy prey. She was always armed. Not with a screwdriver at the moment. But she had her wits about her.

"I would never take anything from you," he said. "I want to build something."

That statement nearly disarmed her. He was a wily one. She'd need to keep her eyes on him. Oh, this man was dangerous. Did she need the money enough to get tangled up with the likes of him?

"We're two grown adults," he said. "Both business savvy from what I can see of your ranch. You were methodical in how you dealt with that loose bull. At least, what I remember of the incident."

His grin went cocky this time. His teeth flashed white at her. Her self-preservation instincts were going haywire. Part of her wanted to run. The confusion was in figuring out the direction. Because most of her body was urging her to crash right into that strong chest and test it for pliability.

"I'm a planner, too," he continued. "Maybe we'd work well together."

Had sexier words ever been uttered by any other man in existence? A man with a plan. And he wanted to partner up. She wondered if he used an old fashioned checklist? Or was he not into paper planners and used a digital organizer on his phone?

Brenda gave herself a shake. Was she seriously talking about marriage? With a stranger? This was not a viable path.

"How can you think we work well together?" she said. "The only evidence we have is from when I told you to stay in the Jeep. You bucked my plan and got out anyway."

Keaton winced. "I didn't understand your plan then. I've told you mine. Tell me yours. Why did you agree to the sale so quickly?"

Brenda swallowed, but the words still escaped her throat. "I need help."

That's not what she'd meant to say. But it came out nonetheless

"I mean the money will help," she tried to course correct. "I've mechanized a lot of the ranch operations. But I still need ranch hands to work with the cattle. And now I'm going to need a new bull for breeding."

"I can help with that," he said. "The hands, I mean. There are six of us. Highly trained Army Rangers. We've been put in tough situations before and came out alive."

"Any of those tough situations happen on a ranch?"

"No, but we're adaptable. Think about it. If we get married, all we'd need is a prenup stating you're entitled to the money for the sale of the creek, and I'm entitled to keep the creek. No other paperwork would be necessary. It's a good plan, and we could both put it into action by the end of the week."

He made it all sound so simple. Brenda would get the money she needed immediately. Plus, free labor. Where was the downside?

CHAPTER NINE

"Hey, Siri, Google what should I include in a prenup?"

"Okay," said the robotic female voice. "Here's what I found with the term prenup."

Keaton winced, as a few heads turned in the coffee shop at Brenda's query. Brenda was entirely oblivious. Her green eyes were completely focused on Siri's findings.

For his part, Keaton was mesmerized by the screen's reflection of Brenda's intent gaze. Her lips pursed as she tapped the screen. She was businesslike as she did her due diligence on her iPhone. When she pulled out a worn memo pad and began making a checklist, Keaton's heart beat so hard he was sure it had turned into a bull ramming to break the fence of his chest.

He was going to marry her. Why didn't that freak him out? It was years ahead of his plan. But she was making a list that ended with the goal of their holy matrimony.

Well, maybe not holy. More like convenient. His convenient bride.

"Looks like we should start by each listing the property we own," she said, turning the page in the memo pad and adding a heading to the new list entitled Owned Property. "And who retains what after the marriage is dissolved."

Dissolved? Keaton took a sip of his tea. The beverage had had time to cool as they sat in the quaint mom and pop coffee shop. But he had trouble swallowing.

"Do you have a planner or any paper to write on?" she asked.

A flush crept over Keaton's cheeks as Brenda regarded him. Her pencil was poised halfway down the sheet of paper where she'd begun making her checklist. He wasn't a paper planner as such. Most times out in the field, a plan wasn't committed to paper. It was discussed, committed to memory, and then executed.

"I don't." He swallowed at the raise in her eyebrows. "I didn't bring any paper with me. I just came to talk to you."

She nodded, closing her memo pad. Keaton balled

his hands into fists, so he wouldn't reach out to stop her. The close of her organized checklist felt like a huge casualty loss.

"It's fine," she said, flicking her thumb over her phone screen. "I can make a shared Google Doc instead."

"Good plan," he said. Was it creepy that he felt a thrill at sharing a virtual space with this woman? A space where they would organize their near futures together. Each day ticking off an item on the list.

She began tapping away. Keaton wrapped his fingers around his styrofoam cup. The tepid tea inside warmed under his palms as he watched Brenda.

Her fingers were long and slender. The nails were ragged. It was clear she was a hard worker.

She glanced up at him. He winced under her gaze. Those green blades of her irises were sharp. Keaton felt he'd been caught staring. Because he had been staring.

"You should note the ranch has debts." Brenda sat her phone aside and laid her hands flat on the table.

"Debts?"

"I've always paid cash, but I needed to upgrade and modernize. The ranch made a lot last year, and projections are good for this year."

She sounded defensive. That was the last thing he wanted her to feel with him. Couldn't she see that he wanted to protect her? To be her defender. He wanted to pull her behind him and fight her battles for her. But with the stiffness in Brenda's upper lip, he knew it would not be appreciated. So, he softened his features and leaned in to listen.

"I could've paid it off," she said. "But I'm shorthanded because my ranch hands were awful. Now, my bull is out of commission."

Her hands rested on the table. Just an inch from his. All he needed to do was reach out to brush her pinky finger, the smallest one. But she balled her hands into fists.

"With the money from the sale, I'll be set right," she said. "So, you see, I wouldn't be a liability."

"Of course, you're not a liability," he said.

Keaton did reach for her hands then. He placed his palm on top of her balled fists. Brenda tensed, tightening her hands like she was putting up her dukes, mounting a defense.

Keaton squeezed. In an instant, the tension seeped out of her hands and into him. Instead of feeling her anxiety, it passed through him, like he was a siphon pulling out the bad and pumping in the good.

Their gazes connected. Green meeting blue. Between them was a horizon that stretched on into eternity. The ground shook when she blinked and pulled her hand away.

"Do you have any debts I should know about?" Brenda asked, picking her phone up again.

Yes. He did. He had experienced an acute loss. But it wasn't financial. Keaton glanced at his empty hands before answering her.

"No. No personal debts. The Army paid for my college. I've lived on a base or been on assignment most of my adult life. So, no credit debt or personal loans. My five partners and I have pooled our resources to start this business."

"Five partners? How do you get anything done with six heads?"

"We're a unit."

"Who's in charge?"

"No one really. We all have the same rank."

Brenda stared at him. Her brow crinkled in confusion. White teeth chewed at her lower lip as though she was trying to work out what he was saying.

"We all have different strengths," he said. "I'm a planner."

"Ah," she sighed as though seeing the answer. "So, you're the overseer."

"That sounds severe."

"It's what I do at the ranch," she said. "I oversee the entire operation. I lay out the tasks and assign them to ranch hands."

Yes, that was pretty much Keaton's role.

"Good. It sounds like we're of a similar mind," Brenda continued. "We should get along during our marriage."

Our marriage. Keaton liked the sound of that. He liked the idea of partnering with Brenda. Working with her. Making a detailed plan with items, and lists, and tasks that they would oversee together.

"When do you think we should schedule the divorce?" Brenda's thumb made a swiping motion. The checklist disappeared and was replaced by a calendar.

Keaton heard the sound of tires screeching in his head. He was back in the Jeep, and another bull had rammed into him. This one was bigger.

"Divorce?" The word was bitter on his tongue. He felt an ache in his left shoulder. His gut churned.

"An annulment wouldn't work because that would negate all of our arrangements," she said.

"Right. No annulment. It has to appear real."

Real like seeing her dressed in white, walking toward him. He'd veto the veil because he'd want to see her eyes. Real like saying vows and making promises. Real like sharing a kiss after being pronounced man and wife.

"Three months?" Brenda said. "You'll be done with your construction and up and running by then."

"No." His voice was harsh. Harsh enough to make her look up from her phone and regard him.

"Four months?" she said.

"No." His voice was softer this time. There was even a ring of reason to his tone. "I mean, we should probably look into it more. Make sure there are no legal holes that might trip us up."

"Good point." Brenda tapped more on her phone. "I've filled out the online prenup template with the information I have. We just need to print it out and sign it."

Keaton rose from his seat. His feet were eager to set this plan in motion. The sooner the paperwork was out of the way, the sooner he could figure out a plan to keep his bride around for longer than four months.

"Actually, wait," said Brenda, still tapping away at her phone.

Keaton did not want to wait. If he'd thought five years was a long time, five days now seemed like an eternity. But he was sure they'd have to wait at least that long to get everything in order for this marriage of convenience.

"I'm looking at the requirements for marriage," said Brenda. "Looks like there's no waiting period in Montana. We could take care of this today."

hen she woke up this morning, the last thing Brenda had planned to do was get married. It was not on her chore list. But here she was with a printed prenup in one hand and a marriage license application in the other.

And it all felt like the most normal thing in the world.

Telling Keaton about her financial strife, planning the near future with him, making lists, it all felt natural. He would make a great ranch hand. Under different circumstances, they might even probably be friends. Since they would be married soon, she supposed maybe they probably should be friends. But that would have to wait until later.

Right now, they needed to fill out this application and get in line at City Hall. Not that there would be a line in this small town. Weddings were family affairs here. She was certain they would be the only people knocking on Judge Perry's door.

"Bren? Is that you?"

Brenda stopped in her tracks at the sound of that voice. Keaton, who'd been keeping step with her since leaving the coffee shop, running into the post office to print the prenup, and then crossing the street to City Hall, bumped into her back at her abrupt halt. His hands came to rest on her forearms and then slid down to cup her elbows.

A shudder went up Brenda's spine. Not a cold sensation. It was like warm sunshine breaking through her blinds in the afternoon. She felt the urge to snuggle back into Keaton's hold. To let him hold her. To let him take the lead.

"Who's your friend?"

Brenda stepped out of Keaton's loose embrace to face off with her brother. "Did you follow me here?"

"I was already here when you came in," said Walter.

"Hmmm. Well, what are you doing here?"

"I asked you first."

The two siblings squared off, coming toe to toe. Though Walter was a man of the Big Guy, he didn't take any sass from his big sister. She was not going to get around him to Judge Perry's office without Walter getting a whiff of what she was on about.

She hadn't considered involving her family in this little manner of her marrying for business reasons. It wasn't really any of their business. They'd all left to pursue their heart's desire. It was only Brenda on the ranch pouring her heart and soul into the running of it. And if she wanted to sell a parcel of the land by leasing her heart and soul, then they had no say in the matter.

"Is there a problem here, Brenda?"

The breath of Keaton's voice touched the tip of her ear. Her shiver would've been evident this time. That is if he hadn't brought her back into his loose embrace. Cupping her elbows once more, his chest lightly touched her shoulder blades. They were definitely firm. She resisted the urge to press her back into his chest to see if there was any give.

"Keaton, this is my brother, Walter."

Keaton's hold on her didn't relax after the announcement of their relationship. Walter extended his hand to Keaton. Keaton released Brenda's elbow and took the proffered hand.

"Pastor Walter Vance," Walter introduced himself formally.

"Pastor?" Keaton's voice, strong a moment ago, sounded a bit choked now.

"Don't let the honorific fool you," said Brenda. "He has a bit of the devil in him."

"Aren't you going to introduce me to your new

friend, Bren?" said her brother with a devilish grin on his face.

"Walter, this is Keaton ... Keaton?"

Oh, wow. She was about to marry this man, and she didn't know his last name. Wait, he'd put it on the prenup. But she didn't dare pull out that document in front of her brother.

"It's Anthony Keaton. Sergeant Anthony Keaton. But everyone calls me Keaton."

"Nice to meet you, Keaton," said Walter. "What are you guys doing here?" He addressed that question to Keaton instead of Brenda.

"What are *you* doing here?" said Brenda.

"Judge Perry is out sick. I was officiating marriages today. But as there are no applications, I was going to head out early."

Walter looked down at her hand. Brenda fought the urge to hide the document behind her back. She was the elder sibling, and she was grown. She didn't have to explain herself to him.

Walter turned his gaze from Brenda and onto Keaton. "You said, Sergeant? You're from the Purple Heart Ranch?"

"Yes," said Keaton. "I'm building a training facility at the border between the two ranches."

"And, let me guess," said Walter. "To stay on the ranch, you need to get married?"

"No." Keaton scratched at his chin. "All the

programs from the training camp won't be longer than six weeks. Meaning everyone involved will be exempt from the family status zoning rule."

"So, you'll only be here for about six weeks?" Walter hedged, clearly still looking for the angle.

"No," said Keaton. "I'm here to stay."

"And where will you live?"

Keaton hesitated. He looked at Brenda. They hadn't talked about that part of their plan.

"With me," Brenda found herself saying. "Keaton and I have come to a business arrangement."

"Business?" said Walter. "What business matter has you holding a marriage license in your hand?"

Brenda jabbed a finger in her brother's chest. "You signed your rights for the ranch over to me, little brother. It's really none of your business."

"As your brother, you're right. It's none of my business. But as the only one qualified to marry anyone today, it very much is my business."

The siblings stared each other down. Brenda gritting her teeth, calculating if she would be forgiven for pinching a man of the church. Walter grinning, clearly loving having the upper hand on his big sister.

"Excuse me, Pastor Vance," said Keaton. "I think you have the right to know that your sister and I are going to enter into a marriage of convenience. We've talked about the pros and the cons, the what-ifs and nots, and we come to an arrangement that will strengthen us both together more than remaining separate entities would accomplish. You have my word that I have Brenda's best interests at heart. I'll never do anything to hurt her because her distress is now my business, and I take my business seriously."

Brenda had fallen back during that speech. She'd turned her body so that she could see Keaton as he made these promises, these vows. Doing that left her future husband and her brother squared off.

Brenda's peaceful, yet annoying, pastor brother and her strong, capable Army Ranger who'd faced down a raging bull regarded each other. It was a formidable pairing.

Brenda hated it, she didn't like being the rope in this testosterone tug of war.

Walter broke into a grin. Keaton stretched out his hand. They clasped hands. Walter brought Keaton in for a hug with a manly clap on the back.

"My prayers have been answered," said Walter.

"Hey!" said Brenda.

"Army Ranger, you said?" said Walter. "You're going to marry my sister, and you're gonna work the land? Man, does God move in mysterious ways."

"It's not real," said Brenda.

"Right," said Walter, brushing his sister's comment away with a wave of his hand as he continued to speak to Keaton. "You got a ring?"

Keaton patted his pocket. But no ring magically

appeared. They'd prepared all of the paperwork, but forgotten that tidbit in their haste to get to City Hall.

"No worries," said Walter. "The judge always has a spare. Follow me."

Keaton put his hand at Brenda's low back as they walked. Brenda meant to step out of his hold. But their steps matched. Since they were keeping the same pace, she let him keep his hand there.

"Uh-huh, found some." Walter produced two plain gold bands from a drawer inside Judge Perry's office. "Ready?"

"Now?" said Brenda and Keaton in unison.

"Would you rather wait until Mom and Dad can fly up here?" said Walter.

"No," said Brenda. "No."

She knew her mother would insist on making a big production of her only daughter's wedding. That planning would take at least three months. They didn't have time for that. Especially when this marriage was barely going to last much longer than that.

"You want the basic package or the deluxe?" said Walter.

"I want whatever would suit Brenda," said Keaton.

Keaton grinned down at her. That wasn't mischief in his gaze. It wasn't him and Walter against her. It was Keaton and her, and there was no foe in front of them. The way was clear.

"Deluxe, it is." Walter cleared his throat. He pursed

his lips and took a deep breath into his nose. He looked upward as though seeking inspiration, much like he did before he began one of his sermons. One of his long sermons. "Marriage, what does that word mean. The scriptures tell us—"

"Switch to the basic package, Walter," snapped Brenda.

Her brother glared at her but complied. "Sergeant Keaton repeat after me."

"I, Anthony Keaton, take thee, Brenda Vance, to be my wedded wife."

Brenda sucked in a breath. As the cool air entered her nose, she tried to slow it down so that it, and the words Keaton repeated, didn't go straight to her head.

"To have and to hold from this day forward, for better, for worse, for richer, for poorer ..."

Well, that was the whole point. This marriage was a means to an end. It would put them both in a better place. It would make them richer instead of poorer.

"To love and to cherish till death do us part."

The breath she'd been holding came out in a gush at that last part. She should've gotten her brother to change that bit. She and Keaton weren't in love. Brenda wasn't even sure if she believed in love. At least not for herself. She'd never had a relationship last long enough that she'd felt cherished.

Keaton took her hands in his. His calloused thumb brushed over her rough knuckles, but somehow the touch was tender. He singled out the fourth finger on her left hand and slid the ring on.

Brenda fought the need to curl her hand into a fist to stop the progression. Once the ring rested at the base of her finger, she felt a heavy weight. Not on her hand. Somewhere else. Somewhere deep in her gut. That feeling in her gut warned her that this ring was not likely coming off.

"Bren," said Walter.

"What?" she snapped.

"Now, it's your turn. Repeat after me."

"I, Brenda Vance, take thee, Anthony Keaton, to be my wedded husband …"

It took Brenda longer to repeat the vows. She needed to keep stopping to take breaths. To swallow. To clear her throat. But finally, she made it to the end.

"To love and to cherish till death do us part." That last part, she got through without incident.

Her fingers shook as she lifted the ring to Keaton's hand. He reached out with his right hand and steadied her grasp. Together, they slid the ring onto the fourth finger of his left hand.

"You may now kiss the bride."

Keaton's gaze dipped to Brenda's lips. Her hand was still in his. He gave her a light tug. Her body came to his without thought. He let one hand go and wrapped his hand on her waist, urging her closer. Again, her body came to him, closing all distance.

With his thumb, he tilted her chin. Her entire face went where he commanded. Lifting to do his bidding.

Since he'd let go of her hands, they were left suspended in the air. She didn't know what to do with them. She rested them on his chest. Well, at least she had confirmation of her suspicions. Behind those strong pecs, were a soft bit of flesh. Like a firm pillow that could offer both comfort and security.

Brenda felt the strength of Keaton's heartbeat. Her own pounding heart slowed, matching his rhythm, falling behind him. His lips were nearly upon hers. She could taste the sugar and lemon from the tea on his breath.

"We don't need to do that part," she said.

"The kiss is a part of the deal," said Walter.

Brenda jerked her head to her nosy brother. "No, it's not."

"Is too," grinned Walter.

Brenda heard a chuckle. Then she felt the warm velvet press on her forehead.

"There," said Keaton as he pulled back from her forehead. "It's sealed."

It was sealed. She was married. She felt like she was the flap of an envelope that had been glued closed. But something got left out. Theoretically, the envelope could be reopened. But part of the flap would be torn and separated. It would never be the same again.

CHAPTER ELEVEN

Keaton pulled out of the rental car company and onto the main street. As he turned the wheel to merge onto the highway, his gaze caught and held on the gold band on his left hand.

What just happened?

He recounted his steps for the day. He'd arrived at the Purple Heart Ranch. He'd met Dylan Banks. The two of them had toured the land. Keaton had driven next door and gotten hit by a bull. And now, he was married.

The honking horn broke his reverie. Keaton slammed his foot on the brake. The action slowed the car, but not his racing pulse. He barely escaped the second collision. This time with an eighteen-wheeler instead of a bull. But catching the side of the truck as it zoomed by, Keaton saw the advertisement for prime beef illustrated in browns, reds, and white.

Haha, fate was funny.

Was this a sign?

He didn't believe in signs. He was the type of man that collected intel, read the data. When all else failed, he trusted his gut.

This marriage was a means to an end. A business arrangement that would benefit them both. It was temporary.

Keaton had left the main street and the town behind and was headed into the countryside, back to the Purple Heart Ranch, where he was meant to stay the night. He looked down the long stretch of road. There was nothing but green pasture for miles, sharp blades of grass. Instead of feeling the razor's edge, his mind kept turning to the smooth, flat part.

Keaton drove on. His foot pressed down on the gas, and he picked up speed. He felt like he'd missed something. Until Vance ranch came into view.

He had missed something, his turn into the Purple Heart Ranch a few miles back. Instead of a U-turn, he made the right turn into the gates. And there she was. His wife.

Brenda rode astride a horse. She was backlit by the setting sun. She looked part warrior, part angel, all his. Even from this distance, Keaton could see the small band on her left hand glinting in the waning sunlight.

From atop her horse, she commanded the cattle, and they obeyed like they were her obedient soldiers. Keaton parked the truck. This time, he'd rented a Ford F150 like hers.

His feet led him to the fencing that separated his wife from him. It was the fencing that the bull had broken through earlier today. It looked like Brenda had put up a temporary barrier. She'd left wood and nails just outside the makeshift railing.

"What are you doing here?"

Keaton looked up. His gaze caught and held on her lips. He'd come so close to kissing those lips just a couple of hours ago. That mission was now moved to the top of his to-do list.

After they'd recited their vows, Keaton's phone had rung. It was the rental car company letting him know there was paperwork for him to sign and a new car to pick out. Brenda had wished him an awkward farewell and took off. Walter, his new brother-in-law, had clapped him on the back and wished him luck, all with that mischievous grin of his. Keaton could only wonder if the man was truly a pastor or an imp in disguise with the way those two bickered.

"Keaton, what are you doing here? I thought you were spending the night at The Purple Heart Ranch."

That's where he'd meant to go. But here he was. The setting sun cast a growing flame around Brenda. Like a moth, he came closer.

"We're married," was all he could think to say.

"Not for real." Brenda swung her leg over the horse to dismount. She held the reins tight in her hand as she settled a hand on the barrier between them.

"I know it's not real." So, why did those words feel like cotton in his mouth? "I just thought we should probably keep up appearances. Not give anyone any reason to question our union."

Their union. Brenda Vance was his wife. No, Brenda Keaton. Mrs. Keaton. She could pretend it wasn't real. But he'd meant every word of the basic vows they'd recited back at City Hall.

Mrs. Keaton frowned with disapproval at her husband. "Exactly what kind of fake marriage do you think this will be?"

Keaton came to her, standing toe to toe. He wanted to scoop her up into his arms. He wanted to press her body against the fence. He wanted to take his first taste of her lips. But there was a rail blocking complete access to her.

"This is the kind of marriage where the husband, that's me, helps out his wife, that's you."

Since he couldn't reach her through the fence, he took the temporary railing down. Then he bent down and picked up the hammer and nails.

"You want to mend fences with me?" she said.

"It was in the vows, for better or worse. The fence needs to be made better."

"There was also that bit about to love and cherish forever," she countered.

Keaton placed a nail. With one strike, the nail made its way through. If only he could get to the heart of his wife as easily. He knew that finding a permanent route into Brenda's heart would take some serious planning with many evasive maneuvers.

"It's just a fence, Bren."

She bristled at the familiar use of her name. She'd have to get used to it. He planned to become very familiar with everything about her in due time. A time frame that would take longer than ninety days. This plan would run for a lifetime.

"You said you needed hands," he said. "I've got two of them that aren't busy right now. Let me help."

Brenda chewed at her lip as he picked up another nail. "Fine. But I'm not going to babysit you. I have too much to do."

"Like I said, it's just the fence. I can handle – ouch!"

The nail slipped. He'd hammered his thumb. Keaton shook out his thumb. But the motion only dispersed the pain.

"Here," Brenda said, dropping the reins of the horse and taking his hand. "Let me see."

Keaton expected her hands to be rough. In some spots, they were. He didn't focus on the rough patches. He honed into where she was tender.

"It's gonna swell," she said. "It'll probably have a shiner. You swung pretty hard."

"Trying to prove to my wife that I'm of use."

Brenda's gaze lifted to his. Something shifted in her green gaze. It was as though a wind blew, and the sharp edge of her eyes turned to the softer, flatter side of the blade. But the wind shifted again, and the look was gone.

"Come on," she sighed. "Help me put the horse away, and then let's ice this up. We need to get the swelling down if I'm going to use those hands."

She turned just as her cheeks reddened. Keaton bit his tongue. Seems they were both of the same mind.

Brenda gave Keaton a tug with one hand. With the other, she grabbed the reins of the horse. Both man and beast moved at her command.

CHAPTER TWELVE

Brenda rolled over, laying her face in her pillow. She hadn't opened her eyes yet. But she knew it was time to get up. She'd never had an alarm clock. Her body just knew.

But this morning she felt languid. She wanted to stay under the covers and snuggle. Gone was the anxious feeling that she had a million things to do. Absent was the disquiet that she had neglected some chore, and the screws were going to fall off her operation. Missing was the panic that she was running late, always running late, before the sun was even up.

The sun wasn't up. But she had to get up. She had a million things to do. She probably had left a chore off her list.

Brenda rolled over onto her back. It was easy to

open her eyes to the new day. Only moonlight showed into her window at this time of day.

Days on a ranch were long in the spring. They began before the sun came up. They ended after the sun went down.

She had cattle to feed. Though the majority of her cattle were strictly grass-fed, she was experimenting with supplemental feeding and watching how it bulked up the cows. It was a project that had put off not only her former ranch hands but her father too. The feeding of cows was a heated subject in these parts.

She would also have to start separating the calves from their mothers soon. They were at the age where they would be branded and taken out to a smaller pasture to start life on their own. It was a bar mitzvah or a sweet sixteen of sorts. Although, instead of getting presents or a new car, they'd get a hot poker and kicked out of their mom's house.

Rubbing a hand over her face, a spot of cold metal went over her forehead and down her nose. The sensation made her shiver. But it wasn't a cold kind of shiver. The prickles running over her skin made her feel warm. When the metallic material got to her mouth, she remembered what it was.

A gold band. A gold wedding band. Because she was married.

There was a creak of the floorboard. The snick of a door opening. The click of a door shutting.

Her husband was awake.

She could hear Keaton moving about the house. He was up already? And she was the slacker still under the covers.

Brenda threw off the covers. She wanted to scramble into clothes and out the door. Unfortunately, she was raised right. She made quick work of tugging her bedsheets into order as her mother had taught her.

By the time the four corners of her bed were maid-service presentable, she heard the *pit-pat* of shower water hitting tiles. She stood in the middle of her bedroom, frozen. Keaton was, as she stood there in her pajamas, in her shower. And if he was like a normal person, he probably wasn't wearing a pair of jeans and a T-shirt in there.

There was a naked man in her shower. And she'd married him. How had she gotten here?

She stared down at the band on her finger. She remembered her brother waving the bands in her face. She remembered the vows both she and Keaton had repeated. Then they'd parted ways, and she hadn't expected to see him again. Until he turned up on her ranch. The rest was a blur.

She'd tended to his thumb. Then she'd offered him some of the leftovers in the fridge because again, she was raised right. Keaton had complimented her on the cooking. She'd accepted the praise. Heating things up to the right temperature was an art, after all.

Brenda had eaten quickly and then begged off. But it had been late. She'd pointed out a room down the hall. Then she'd shut herself into her room. And locked the door. Only to unlock it a second later.

Keaton might be a stranger. But he was her husband. She might not know him well, or at all. But she knew he wouldn't hurt her.

The shower had stopped during her trip down memory lane. Good. He was done. She could slip into the bathroom, then out the door, thus avoiding any need to face him.

With that plan formed, Brenda opened the bedroom door to head to the bathroom. But as she stepped out of her bedroom, Keaton stepped out of the bathroom.

His hair was spiked up. His face was scrubbed clean. There was no sleep in his alert gaze. There was also no shirt covering his bare chest.

Tanned skin was stretched over a six-pack of hard, lean muscle. No, scratch that. There was an eight-pack there. Was that a thing? It clearly was since Brenda was looking at it, staring at it.

"Good morning."

"Huh?" said Brenda.

"You might want to give it a second to cool off before you jump in," he said.

"I wasn't going to—" Her gaze shot up and met with sparkling blue mischief. "What?"

"The shower," said Keaton. "I like it hot. So, there's a lot of steam in there."

"Steam?"

His grin was slow, wicked like he knew where her mind had gone. It hadn't gone anywhere. It was stuck on the man in front of her with his steamy eight-pack, the damp towel draped low on his hips, and his bare feet.

Large, bare feet. You know what they say about men with large feet. Big boots.

"Brenda?" Those large, unbooted feet took a step toward her, and then another. A lean finger reached out for her. Keaton tilted her chin up so that she was looking directly in his eyes. "You good?"

"Hmmm?"

Keaton kept his index finger under her chin. With his thumb, he rubbed at the space under her eyes. "You sleep okay?"

"Hmmm?"

From the hall window, the sun stretched its first rays up from the horizon. The tendril of warmth heated Brenda's cheek. But not as much as the heat from the clear blue gaze of the man who was cupping her cheek.

"You have a long chore list today?" he asked.

"Hmmm. I mean, yes. Feed to grind. Manure to shovel. Fences to mend."

"Hmmm."

Keaton's gaze was on her lips. His index finger still held her chin. Which was a good thing. She was certain that single finger was the sole thing holding her up in the world as she could no longer feel her legs. All sensation had gone to her lips.

She felt completely oversensitive. She needed something to soothe the rising ache that zinged from her upper lip to her lower lip. She flicked her tongue out to moisten them.

Big mistake.

The moisture only served to make her lips even more swollen. Like a balloon that had one too many breaths blown into it. Brenda felt like she was going to pop if she didn't get relief soon.

And the only relief she wanted was the pair of lips that were coming closer and closer—

Ding dong.

The ringing of the doorbell broke them apart. They both looked down the stairs at the door to the house.

"You're far more presentable than I am," said Keaton, his hand waving in front of the damp towel that kept him somewhat modest.

Brenda turned and took the stairs on wobbly legs. By the time she reached the last rung, she had her wits about her again.

Keaton was a distraction. This marriage was a means to an end. She had to get his glistening chest out of her mind and off of her ranch. She had far too much work to do.

Opening the door, she was met with two large male bodies. Unlike Keaton, they were fully clothed. But like Keaton, they had that air about them that reeked of soldier. She turned away from the newcomers and back to the stairs.

"Honey, it's for you."

CHAPTER THIRTEEN

"Working the plan, huh?" said Grizz.

"There were some unforeseen complications," said Keaton as he shut the door and ushered his two friends out.

Grizz and Mac had stared up at him in his towel while Brenda stood in her pajamas on the doorstep. Brenda had offered the men coffee while Keaton had thrown on his clothes. In that time, he knew his men had made up their own minds about what they had seen.

"She looks like a very complex set of curves a man could get lost in," said Mac.

"Hey." Keaton shoved the other man. Mac could've easily dodged the jab, but Keaton's next words stopped him cold. "That's my wife you're talking about."

"Your wife?" both Mac and Grizz said in unison.

"Yeah." Keaton scrubbed his hand through his hair. His fingers caught in the strands. He was due for a cut soon.

"As in married?" asked Mac.

"Yeah," said Keaton. He should probably find a barber in town. Or maybe there was someone next door at the Purple Heart Ranch who did buzz cuts. He'd rather have his hair cut by a soldier than someone he didn't know.

"You been here less than forty-eight hours," said Grizz. "Barely twenty-four."

"And you're not on the Purple Heart Ranch land where this kind of thing is expected," said Mac.

"Like I said," shrugged Keaton, "there was a complication."

"That required a wife?" asked Grizz. His voice was more growl than anything.

Keaton would've expected the push back from Mac, who'd been eager to walk down the aisle since before he'd joined the service. Definitely from Rusty, who was separated from his wife, whom Keaton was sure the man was still in love with. He couldn't understand why Grizz was giving him the push back.

"Yeah," said Keaton. "It's the creek; it's not a part of the land deal with Banks. It belongs to Brenda – that's my wife. This is her land. But the only way we could get past all the restrictions to purchase the land and begin construction was if I was an owner. So, we decided the easiest way was to get married."

The two men stared at him. Mac's mouth worked like he was trying to say something. But no actual words escaped his lips. Grizz simply glared, his nose wrinkled like he smelled something foul.

A door opening and slamming turned Keaton's attention from his men. It was the back door to the house. They each turned to see Brenda, clad in form-fitting jeans, a tank top that hugged those curves Mac should not be noticing, and a cowboy hat on her head, jog down the backstairs. She tipped her hat to them all before heading toward the nearest barn.

Keaton forgot what he was saying as he watched her walk. The woman moved like she was a general, and all in her sight were under her command. Before she got too far away, Keaton saw her reach for something in her back pocket. She pulled out the memo pad. Tugging a pencil from the coils at the top of the pad, she began making marks.

"Easiest way, huh?" said Grizz.

Keaton bit at his lower lip. The sun hadn't fully risen in the sky, but he was suddenly parched. He'd kill for a tall, cool glass of green tea.

"You're really married?" Grizz grabbed for Keaton's left hand. He studied the band on his finger, pressing his thumb over it like he was testing it for realness.

The guilt settled in now. All of the men in his unit

looked upon each other as though they were brothers. But Keaton was the closest thing to family that Grizz had. They'd grown up together. Grizz had spent many a night at the Keatons' dinner table and sleeping in a pile of covers on Keaton's bedroom floor. Grizz's home life had been less than ideal.

They'd done almost everything together, including joining the military. Keaton had always assumed that Grizz would've been the best man at his wedding. Only his wedding had been yesterday, and his best friend hadn't been at his side. But Grizz didn't seem entirely put out by it if the grin on his face was any proof.

"You tell your mom?" asked Grizz.

Keaton gulped. His gut shriveled in his belly. His shoulders developed an ache like when he was a scrawny kid back in gym class facing the pull-up bar. Suddenly, he felt four feet tall again.

Grizz cupped his ear and leaned into Keaton. "What was that?"

Keaton cleared his throat to try to make the sound louder. "No," he squeaked.

Grizz threw his head back and laughed. The sound was what a grizzly bear would make before it took its prey's head off. "You're a dead man."

"Well," said Mac, "at least you got to experience love before you died."

"Love?" said Keaton. "It's not like that."

"Maybe not for her yet. But for you?" Mac looked Keaton up and down. "Oh, yeah, it's like that."

Mac Kenzie would know. He'd been in love nearly all his life. With the same woman. But it hadn't worked out the first time. Or the second time. Or the dozens of other times he'd professed his undying love to her after that. Mac had always said that, for him, love was instant and then forever.

Was Keaton in love with Brenda? Had it been instant? The first time he'd seen her, he'd felt the earth move. True, a bull had rammed into him.

He'd been attracted to women before. He'd cared about a few. But those caring feelings had been a faucet left trickling a stream of water. With Brenda, Keaton felt he could barely keep his head above the title wave of water that crashed into him whenever he was near her.

"Yeah," Keaton sighed. "It's like that."

"So, the rumors about this place are true." Mac turned from Keaton to Grizz. "You're gonna get hitched, too."

Grizz didn't back up. He held his ground. "I'm not superstitious. And I'm not marriage material."

"Tell that to Patty."

"What does my sister have to do with anything?" said Keaton.

Mac made a scoffing sound. "You do realize she's in love with him."

"It's just a silly crush." Keaton brushed the notion away. It was normal for little sisters to have crushes on their brother's best friends. But that was years ago. His sister was in college, and she had a boyfriend.

"Patty Cakes is not a little girl anymore," said Mac.

"Hey!" Keaton and Grizz both growled at Mac.

Before the two men could advance, Mac held up his hands in surrender. "What? You both realize I'm taken."

"By a woman who keeps running away from you," said Grizz.

"She's not running," said Mac. "She just has cold feet."

"For almost a decade?" said Keaton.

"I'm giving her time to warm up to the idea," said Mac.

"This doesn't change anything," said Keaton. "We still need to get the camp finished in ninety days. And ... I promised we'd help Brenda with a few chores around here."

"What?" said Grizz. "So, we're ranchers now?"

CHAPTER FOURTEEN

She had been infiltrated. The ranch was under attack. The insurgents were everywhere.

After taking a cold shower in the hot bathroom, Brenda still hadn't gotten the feel of Keaton's fingertips on her face out of her mind. Her mind kept insisting that he had kissed her. She couldn't shake the certainty that she knew what his lower lip felt like, what his upper lip tasted of. It was as though his fingers had transferred the memories directly into her head.

Brenda shoveled a load of manure. But even the rank smell didn't clear her head. She was already behind for the day, for the week, because of all she had to deal with for her former ranch hands' incompetency. And now from Keaton's hands, which had wound up on her body.

She had to set boundaries for this marriage. Boundaries that were drawn at arm's length. Problem was, she'd have to actually come face to face with her husband to make those edicts. For now, she was avoiding him.

It was past lunchtime, and she'd seen not hide nor hair of Keaton. But she knew he was near. Her body felt like an antenna that was picking up his frequency. She felt a constant low hum of his energy. She needed more activity to shuck the excess off.

She should get started on separating the calves for branding. But she turned from that pasture and headed for the bull's pen. Luckily, there was always a fence to be mended on a ranch.

When she came to the broken fence that Manuel had kicked down, and Keaton had lost a fight with a hammer, she saw it was repaired. The big soldier, the one that looked like a bear, was putting away the hammer and nails. His large hands looked untouched by the hammer's face.

"What are you doing?" she asked.

The man straightened to his full height. Which rivaled that of a grizzly bear. He was broad as a bear too, blocking out the midday sun.

"Brenda, right?"

His voice sounded like he'd swallowed a bear. It was low and deep. Brenda felt certain that if he ever shouted, the sound would likely shake the ground.

"Name's Griffin. But everyone calls me Grizz."

"I can see why."

He didn't smile. He regarded her with complete suspicion. Well, he needed to learn she'd faced down … well, maybe not larger men. But she needed Grizz to know that she didn't scare easily, no matter how big her opponent.

"What are you doing, Griffin?"

The only indication he gave that he caught her snub of friendship was the slight raise of his left eyebrow. "Keaton said the fence needs mending. So, I took care of it."

"You didn't have to do that," she said.

"You're Keaton's wife. He's my brother."

"Which makes me your sister?"

Now the right brow lifted to meet the left one. But he still didn't break into a smile or break eye contact with her. This was a test of dominance. Well, this big bear was about to find out that Brenda never blinked first.

"It makes you a part of this team," Grizz concluded.

Brenda gasped. Taking a step back, she blinked at those words. "It's … me and Keaton … we're… it's not real. It's just temporary."

Once again, Grizz held her there under his unblinking, unrelenting, unsmiling glare. For the first time in her life, Brenda squirmed. Not in fear of this man. She squirmed at the lie that had just left her lips.

"Once a Ranger, always a Ranger," said Grizz. "That goes for family, too. Wives, especially. Sisters, too."

With that last statement, Grizz finally broke his glare. But not before Brenda caught something flash in his hard gaze. Something that made his hazel eyes go soft. Brenda opened her mouth to argue but felt it would be a waste of breath.

"Grizz?"

He lifted his head to look back at her.

"Wear a hat," she said. "Or the sun will burn you up."

He lifted an eyebrow but nodded his head. His lip curled. It wasn't exactly a smile. But it wasn't exactly a frown either. "Yes, ma'am."

Brenda walked away from the bear of a man. There were still many chores to check off her list and a shortage of hands to get the work done. There was feed to grind for her special herd of cattle. But when she got to the grinder, the other soldier was there.

"Afternoon, Mrs. Keaton."

Like Keaton and Grizz, this guy was also built like a truck. But unlike the grizzly bear, this man wore a friendly, almost infectious grin on his handsome face.

"It's Brenda."

"I'm Mac Kenzie."

"Mackenzie?"

"Close enough." He shrugged. "You can call me Mac."

"Nice to meet you, Mac. What are you doing?"

"Keaton said I needed to grind the feed." He turned to her new machine, technology which her former hands hadn't deigned to touch. "I Googled how to do it."

Mac patted the machine, which was purring like a kitten as it churned out the goods. It was exactly how Brenda wanted it done. She returned Mac's grin. She decided she liked this one.

"Where's Keaton?" she asked.

"Your hubby said he was cleaning corrals. Whatever that means."

Brenda turned to head in that direction. Mac put a hand to her forearm to stop her.

"Hey, Brenda, welcome to the team." With a wink and a nod, Mac turned back to his work.

A few moments later, Brenda found Keaton. He'd taken his shirt off but was in his undershirt. The white shirt had dirt smudges and spots of sweat in some places.

Brenda didn't focus on those. She got a clear view of his biceps as he set about his work. With his back to her, she was mesmerized by the movement of his shoulder blades and back muscles.

As though he sensed her presence, Keaton turned and caught her staring. Brenda had the urge to run and hide. But she held her ground.

This was her ranch. They'd invaded her space. She

was in charge here. Even though these three Army Rangers were doing everything she needed done, the way she wanted it done.

"Everything okay?" Keaton asked.

Brenda had to swallow down a huge lump in her throat before she could respond. She wondered if that lump was her pride. "It's perfect."

Keaton's grin spread wider. He took a step toward her. Brenda took a deep breath and forced more hard to say words from her lips.

"Thank you for your help."

Keaton took another step closer to her.

"I really appreciate it." With one more step, they were toe to toe. "But shouldn't you be getting started on your camp?"

"Change of plans," Keaton said. "I told the guys to put your to-do list first."

"Won't that set you back?" If she reached out, her fingers would meet his bicep and come away damp from the sweat of his hard work.

"We'll catch up. I'm working with six pairs of hands and eighty-nine days. You were completely shorthanded."

There was electricity buzzing between them. That hum that she'd been trying to avoid all day was zinging around her head, in the palm of her hand, in the balls of her feet. More and more, she was feeling powerless against it.

"But now I've got you," she said.

Keaton nodded. "You've got me."

"I haven't been part of a team in a while. It's just been me since my family left the ranch."

"We're your family now." Keaton's hand came up to cup her cheek. They were back where they'd left off this morning. "Hey, Brenda?"

"Yeah, Keaton?"

With her head cradled in his palm, he tilted her head back. The brim of her hat could no longer hide her from him. She felt completely exposed.

"I was thinking," he continued, "maybe I could take you out to dinner? To get to know each other better."

"You mean like a date?"

"Yeah," he grinned. "Call me crazy, but I'd like to take my wife on a date. What do you say?"

Brenda knew she should say no. It wasn't that kind of marriage. It was business. And now he wanted to mix pleasure in. And, oh man, did she want to mix things all up.

She wanted to take a leap with a man like Keaton. Because a man like Keaton would be there to catch her. Heck, he'd likely make plans to be certain she would never fall in the first place.

He'd delegate others to watch out for her. He'd stick around until the job was done. He wouldn't leave her behind. Apparently, it was in the creed.

Brenda opened her mouth to accept when his

phone buzzed. The buzz wasn't the normal ring of a cellphone. It was a catchy tune, the kind that would be programmed for a specific caller. It took Brenda a second to place it because she wasn't a *Star Wars* fan, but she was almost certain that was the death march song for the villain of the film, Darth Vader.

Keaton cringed as he jerked his hand away from Brenda. He shoved his hand in his pocket, pulling out his cell phone. He looked at the phone and cringed again.

"I have to get this," he said. "But before I do, I just want to say I'm sorry."

Keaton inhaled and let the breath out slowly. He held the phone to his ear. Then seemed to think better of it because he held the device away from his ear before pressing the Talk button.

"You're married!" The shrill voice carried over the receiver to fill the space between them.

"Hey, Mom."

CHAPTER FIFTEEN

Keaton's ear was still ringing from his mother's tongue lashing over the phone. He was sure he knew how she'd found out about his impromptu wedding. Grizz had to know to expect a stealth attack coming his way. Keaton had barely been able to get a word into the conversation.

Not that it had been much of a conversation.

With his father sent on deployment after deployment, Keaton's mom had taken on much of the rearing of her two kids. Having to play both roles, the matriarch and the patriarch, the good cop and the bad cop, the one who cooked dinner and also played catch, Holly Keaton had developed some extra special talents. His mom didn't just have eyes in the back of her head like a normal disciplinarian. No, she could sense when her kids were misbehaving a few blocks away. And when she came to find them, Keaton and his sister Patty always swore they heard the trumpets blaring Darth Vader's *Imperial March*.

"Are you grounded?"

The back door hit him in the rear as he stepped over the threshold. Brenda leaned one hip against the counter as she sipped on what had to be her fifth cup of coffee for the day. Keaton had the urge to take the cup from her hands and replace the ceramic lip of the mug with his own.

The day was over. The sun had set. The only work that needed to be done was the work of slipping under his wife's defenses to get to the heart of her.

"Yup, I'm grounded." Keaton took the steps to close the distance between him and Brenda. But he didn't reach for her cup. She was clearly a caffeine addict. The only way to get rid of one addiction was to replace it with another. "I'm afraid I can't take you to the school dance this weekend."

Brenda giggled. The movement had her lower the cup from her lips on her own. "That's a harsh penalty for a grown man who got married without his mommy's permission."

"I'm sure she'll forgive us after the first grandkid."

The cup slipped from her hands. Keaton reached out and caught it before it hit the floor. He looked up to find Brenda's cheeks reddening. Keaton knew his response was to take the comment back. But he couldn't set his mouth to do it.

"Did you tell your parents?" he asked.

"I will."

Keaton set the half-drunk coffee mug into the sink. "I know you plan for this to be temporary—"

"We," Brenda corrected him. "We plan for this to be temporary."

"Right," he said. "But your family should know what we're up to. You don't want to get in trouble like me."

She turned her face away from him, looking out the large kitchen window at the last rays of the setting sun. "My family isn't concerned about what goes on here. They all scattered as soon as they could and left me in charge."

Keaton reached out to her then. He picked up where they'd left off outside. He lifted her cheek with his index finger. Her green gaze met his. The color of her eyes wasn't the sharp blade of grass now. It was the flat side after a lawnmower, or tractor, or booted foot cut it down.

There was pain in the crinkle of her eyes. Keaton felt the sharpness of the hurt, almost as if it had happened to him. He wanted to take it away from her. He wanted to swallow it down. Toss it away. Whatever it would take to keep it away from her. All he could do was rub his thumb tenderly at the corner of her eye. His tenderness broke her silence.

"I love being in charge," she said.

"Yeah, I got that impression."

She smiled, which caused her eyes to crinkle in a different way now. "I was born to run this place, and I've done a very good job of it."

"I can see that. This operation looks well planned out with clear tasks and objectives to reach an achievable goal."

Brenda preened under his compliments. Her cheeks spread even wider as she grinned. Her warm flesh filled the palm of Keaton's hand as he continued to cradle her face.

And then it was gone. The smile and the light in her eyes blinked out. Her head lowered, coming out of Keaton's grasp.

"My dad's heart just wasn't in this place anymore. He never wanted to be a rancher. He did it for his dad, for his family. Grandpa always said family first."

There was more to that statement. But she didn't say it. She didn't need to. Looking around the kitchen table where eight chairs were evenly spaced around the dining table, it was clear to see that her family wasn't here any longer. Neither were the ranch hands she hired. No one was here for her.

Keaton wanted to wrap Brenda up in his arms. He wanted to lift her chin again and let her know she didn't need to hold it high on her own anymore.

Because he was there for her. He'd always be there for her. Temporary was not going to do it for him.

He reached for her. Not her chin. He reached for her elbow. With a tug, she came willingly.

She let him wrap an arm around her shoulders. Her shoulders were stiff, but some of the weight dropped as Keaton pressed his palm's into her shoulder blades. He cradled the back of her head, preparing to tuck her under his chin. But she didn't lower her head. She looked up at him.

Keaton's gaze dipped to her lips. They were parted. The tip of her tongue dipped out to moisten her lower lip.

Keaton was excellent at reading signs in a combat zone. He often got his signals crossed when it came to women and the mixed messages that they sent. Not his Brenda. The messages she was sending were clear. He could cross the bridge. He could kiss her.

He would kiss her. Not a temporary peck. He was going to kiss this woman every day. For the rest of their lives. Starting now.

The back door banged open. Grizz and Mac stormed over the threshold like invaders launching an unexpected, unwelcome attack. Brenda ducked out of Keaton's hold, leaving him feeling shell-shocked.

"Are we indentured servants, or are we going to get fed?" asked Mac.

"I'm neither a maid nor a short order cook," said Brenda.

"Lucky for you, I'm a metrosexual," said Mac.

Brenda held up her hands. "Oh, I don't judge."

Grizz broke into a grin. Keaton noted it was the first time his best friend had cracked a smile since arriving on the ranch. He should ask what was up. But only after he got in a shot for coming between him and his wife.

"It means that I'm a heterosexual male who is not afraid to show my feminine side," said Mac.

Brenda still looked confused.

"It means I'll cook."

Mac headed to the fridge to survey the stores. Grizz turned to the cupboards in search of pots.

"We've already washed up," said Mac. "Why don't you two get cleaned up while we prepare a feast."

Keaton followed Brenda up the stairs. Halfway up, he stopped pretending that he wasn't enjoying the view. She was his wife. What was his was hers, and what was hers would soon be his. If he played his cards right. And Keaton was certain he was figuring out the rules of this game.

"What's on the agenda tomorrow?" he asked.

Brenda turned in the hall just outside her door. "Agenda?"

"Your checklist." Keaton canted his head. He

couldn't see the imprint of the memo pad that had shaped the back of her jeans. But the impression of it from him staring all the way up the stairs was burned in his mind. "Tell me, what do you need doing tomorrow?"

"Oh, nothing," said Brenda. "You have your hands full—"

"Didn't we just have this conversation outside? My brothers and I are here to help. You're family now. Your list is my list."

She chewed at that lower lip, but it didn't hide the smile that lifted one side of her face. Keaton's stomach grumbled. But he wasn't hungry for whatever Mac was whipping up downstairs. All he wanted to take a bite out of was the woman in front of him. Starting with that plump lip.

"Our agreement made me part owner in this land," he said. "A small part, yes. But I'm here to stay. Whatever happens between us, I'm not leaving."

Again her lips parted, giving him the universal sign to fire at will.

"Do you want something to happen between us, Bren? Because I—"

His last words were cut off as Brenda's lips crashed into his. Her lips were a curious probe. They tread softly, covering the area of his bottom lip.

Keaton launched a full attack. He brought one hand to her low back and pressed her to him. The other hand, he used to cup the back of her head, angling her mouth for maximum devastation.

But the plan backfired. He'd meant to overwhelm her defenses. Quickly, he saw that he was in the danger zone with this woman.

Through all her outward armor, she was soft and pliable in his hold. At his first strike, she yielded. The thing was, Keaton had crossed into this territory with a white flag of surrender. He'd had no intention of putting up a fight.

He opened to her, letting her invade his senses. Letting her invade his mind. Letting her invade his heart.

The organ in his chest changed its tune and fell into step with her. His every sense was tuned to the tenderness of her touch, the sweetness of her scent, the spicy note at the corner of her upper lip. His mind rearranged its masterplan to do her bidding, starting with that memo pad. His fingers grazed as they slipped from her low back to the pocket of her jeans.

Keaton broke the kiss. He was gratified to see that Brenda clung to him as she tried to recover her wits. Keaton already had his wits about him, and he had her list in his hands.

"If you won't tell me what you need, I'll just have to look for myself."

He opened the pad to find organized lists with checkmarks beside each one. There were dates at the top of each page. When he flipped the page, he didn't see a listing for tomorrow's date.

"I told you," said Brenda, her voice still breathy from their kiss. "There's nothing to do tomorrow. Tomorrow is Sunday. Church."

"Well," said Keaton. "I'll be there."

CHAPTER SIXTEEN

There was a boy in her bedroom.

Brenda had moved into her parents' bedroom after they'd retired. But she'd always felt it was too large for her. She'd purchased a new mattress, but often felt swallowed up by the queen-sized bed. She'd moved out most of their old furniture and felt like she was on an island at the center and needed to send out an SOS.

But she'd outgrown her old room. And she was now the sole owner of this big house. So, of course, she'd taken the biggest bedroom.

She'd brought her clothes and her dresser in there. She'd painted the room in a shade of blue that was supposed to be good for sleep. Looking around the room, she realized that that shade of blue was the exact color of Keaton's eyes.

Keaton, her husband. Keaton, the man who had been sleeping in her bedroom for the past two nights. Her childhood bedroom which was just two doors down the hall.

His large body would certainly fall over the frame of her full-size bed. His muscular arms would likely crush the soft pillows at the head of her bed. His bare feet would slip out of her old comforter.

The man was simply too much for her old room. He belonged in a room the size of her parents' old room. She'd bet if he were in there with her, it wouldn't feel so large. She'd bet it'd feel just right.

She heard the familiar creak of the door of her old bedroom. She heard the floorboards take on the weight of a full-grown soldier. Brenda's breath caught and held as Keaton's footsteps made their way down the hall toward her.

Was he coming in here?

Coming back to finish what he'd started last night just outside this room?

Well, technically, she had started it.

She had no idea what had possessed her to reach up and kiss him. She might be bossy on the ranch, but she was not that girl out in the dating field. She really hadn't had that much experience out in the world of dating. She had always been far too busy on the ranch. And most men didn't appreciate a woman in what was traditionally a man's job.

Except Keaton. He didn't have a problem with her being the boss. In fact, she was almost certain his blue eyes sparkled every time she pulled out her checklist. He seemed eager for her to give him a task to complete.

Yet when she'd taken charge of his lips, he'd expertly slipped the reins of control from her and taken charge. Brenda's lips still burned from their kiss last night. Even surrounded by the calming, blue walls, her body had been far too primed for sleep.

When she heard the bathroom door open, her hand touched her lips that were swollen with want. When she heard the shower turn on, her fingers slid down her heated cheeks. Her hand continued down her throat, which was parched even though a full glass of water sat on her bedside table. Her hand ended at her belly, which grumbled even though she wasn't hungry.

Brenda put her feet on the ground. She was not one to get carried away by a man. She was a strong woman. So, why did her knees wobble as she stood?

She padded to the door and eased it open. The *pitter-patter* of water let her know Keaton was still occupied in the shower. On light feet, she made her way down the hall to her old room.

Even though it was her old room, she knew that opening the door would be an invasion into her guest's privacy. Luckily, the door was cracked open.

Brenda peered inside. The walls in there were a shade of green, which was also said to promote sleep. But the green walls had only made Brenda think of the outside and her chores, and what she had to get checked off her list the next day. All of which meant she hadn't slept much in there.

On the wall hung a picture of her family. Her mom and dad stood together, their arms around each other. Her brother's hand rested on the cross at his neck, his gaze tilted upwards. And there she was, looking off to the side at the ranch.

Brenda didn't doubt for a second that her parents loved her. She knew they believed in her too. She knew with certainty from how frequently her brother was in her kitchen, making sure she was fed, that she had Walter's love and support for what she was doing with her life. But none of them wanted a hand in the family business. It was only her two hands.

Brenda looked away from the family portrait. It was the only thing left in this room that was hers. Everything else belonged to Keaton.

She noted that the bed was made. The sheets pulled tight to the corners like a hotel maid had visited. A green and brown military bag sat at the foot of the bed.

Brenda took a step closer. She knew that opening the bag and peering inside would be the height of ill manners. Luckily, the bag was open.

Inside, she saw a stack of folded clothes in one corner. In the other corner of the bag were two photos. One image was of six men. All in fatigues. All grinning at the off-screen photographer. Three of the grinning faces she recognized.

The other photo was of Keaton and a woman. Again, he grinned at the camera with those sparkling blue eyes of his. Looking closer, she saw that there was a hint of exasperation in the up-tilt of his lips. The girl, a redhead, grinned at him. She had her arms around his neck. Her chin tilted up like she expected to be kissed.

Was this an old girlfriend? Maybe it was his current girlfriend. Whatever she was, it was clear that she was important to him. She had a place in his well-organized bag.

"Hey."

Brenda jolted. One hand went over her racing heart. The other covered her mouth to hold in her yelp of surprise. Here she stood in the middle of her old bedroom in a cami and a pair of men's boxer shorts. The boxers were more comfortable than the flannel when it got warm in the big house.

Unlike the previous morning, Keaton, unfortunately, was dressed. His firm cushion of a chest was covered by a pressed white shirt. Those powerful thighs that made a damp towel look like the height of fashion were draped in dark slacks.

"Am I overdressed?" he asked.

"No," she said, taking her hand from her mouth as she stared. "You look great."

"Thanks," he grinned. "You, too. I'm a lucky man if my wife wakes up looking like this."

Brenda was not the type of woman whose tongue got tied. Except with this man. She swallowed down the knot in her stomach and pushed forth what needed to be said.

"Do you have a girlfriend?"

Keaton lifted a brow at her. Then he lifted his hand and placed it on her waist. With the gentlest of tugs, Brenda came to him. Her body went, but her gaze stayed on the picture in the bag. She had to stay focused.

Keaton's gaze followed hers to the bag. He grinned like a man with a secret he was itching to tell. But he held his tongue.

"No," he said. "I don't have a girlfriend. I have a wife."

"Do you have an ex-girlfriend you're not over?" Brenda prodded.

"No," he said. "There's never been anyone I wanted to hold onto."

His grip tightened around Brenda's waist. His thumbs rubbed tight circles in her sides, making her feel dizzy. The motion loosened her tongue.

"What about the picture in your bag?" she said.

"Picture?" For a man that spoke his mind since the moment she'd met him, Keaton's voice was full of fake innocence.

"All right," she said, pounding a hand against his chest. "I was snooping. But it's my house."

"Our house." His hands came to her back, and he pressed her deeper into the comfort of his chest.

But Brenda stiffened her arms, unwilling to cave into the warmth she knew was at the heart of this man. "Is that what this is? You just want my property?"

"That was what it was about. A means to an end. A convenient arrangement. But I told you, I want more."

Without warning, and without any real protest from her, Keaton claimed Brenda's lips. Her stiff arms collapsed. Her fingers curled around his neck. They had to. She needed something to hang onto as he deepened the kiss and wiped all her good sense away.

"She's my sister," he said when he let her up for air.

"Who?" It took Brenda a second to open her eyes. The world was spinning off its axis. Luckily, she had something strong and reliable to hold onto; Keaton.

"The redhead in the photo. In the bag you were snooping in. She's not my girlfriend. She's not my ex. She's my sister. I'm a one-woman kind of man."

Brenda leaned back and looked into those clear blue eyes. She didn't believe in fate. She believed in a good plan. She'd researched that color of blue that was on her walls. The hue had definitely had a good effect on her this past year. She'd never felt more rested than when she closed her eyes after staring at those walls.

"And," Keaton continued, "I'll have you know that I'm happily dating my wife. You'd better get ready for church, Mrs. Keaton."

With another light press to her mouth, he was gone. Brenda stood in her childhood bedroom and felt like a stranger. Keaton had driven into her life and knocked everything off-kilter.

Even though things weren't going according to her original plan, she felt certain she was on the right path. She had a man who didn't challenge her every thought. Instead, he sought out her advice and consulted her on the way forward for both of them.

And it wasn't just him. He had a team that was loyal to him. And now they were loyal to her by extension. They were going to stay and work the land. For the first time in a long time, Brenda had a team she could rely on.

CHAPTER SEVENTEEN

Keaton couldn't stop rubbing at his bottom lip. The taste of Brenda, his wife, still lingered there long moments after he'd released his hold on her. In his mind, he rearranged every plan he had to date. Now, written in black ink at the top of his master plan, was to have more of her as soon as possible, as often as possible, as long as possible.

"We have a problem," said Grizz.

Keaton was used to hearing those four words in his former line of work. Nothing ever went exactly according to plan on a mission. Typically, when someone said that phrase, his ears went alert. His mind would start buzzing as he mentally made alterations to his plans.

His mind buzzed, all right. But it was more like

butterflies flitting around in his head. He wondered what his wife would wear today for church. He wondered if he should introduce her with his last name attached. Though she lived in a fairly traditional town, she had all the hallmarks of a modern woman.

Would she want to keep her own last name? Maybe she'd want to hyphenate? But whose name would she want first? Vance-Keaton or Keaton-Vance? And would he follow suit and change his name? He would if that's what their children would be named.

"Rusty got held up," Grizz continued. "All he would say is it was a family matter, and he'd get here as soon as possible."

"Well, he should take care of that," said Keaton. "Family should come first."

Keaton didn't miss Grizz and Mac's shared look. He just wasn't too interested in figuring out what that look meant. His attention was turned to the stairs as he awaited Brenda's appearance.

"That means we're a man down," said Mac. "It means it's going to set us behind."

"Oh, you're right." The mention of the time frame snapped Keaton out of his stupor. "And now, with the ranch chores, it will set us behind even more."

Keaton rubbed at his chin as he tried to rework the two schedules in his head. He assumed Grizz and Mac were pondering the same logistics when they exchanged another narrow-gazed look.

"You do realize we can't do both and make the schedule," said Grizz.

Keaton removed his fingers from his chin and crossed his arms. "We have to. I promised my wife."

"I thought you said this marriage wasn't real," said Grizz. "Something about a means to an end."

"I never said that." Keaton took a step toward his oldest friend.

"What you definitely said was that you would have this camp ready in a crazy quick time period." Grizz took a step toward Keaton. "You gave your word, and by extension, all of our words. A Ranger does not go back on his word."

"Neither does a husband."

"A real one wouldn't." Grizz met that step until they were toe to toe.

"This is real." Keaton leaned forward until they were nose to nose.

A set of hands came between the two men. Mac gave each a push. When that didn't work, he shoved his body between them.

"Is there a problem?" said a female voice.

The three men turned their heads. All tension left the room as they looked up toward the top of the stairs. Keaton forgot about his friend's aggression. He forgot about the need to rearrange his plans. He forgot how to breathe.

Brenda stood at the top of the stairs. He'd only seen

her in either jeans and boots, or in boxers and barefoot. Brenda standing in a simple sundress and sandals made Keaton go stupid.

"You look amazing, Brenda," said Mac.

"Yeah, you look really pretty." There was a gruffness to Grizz's voice like he was annoyed that he spoke the truth.

Keaton was annoyed with them both. They'd given her two of the best compliments. What was left for him to say?

"She's mine," Keaton growled.

Brenda had taken her first step down the stairs. But at Keaton's words, she halted. Her shoulders rotated as though she were about to take a step back. Keaton walked to the landing. He extended his hand up to her and waited.

When her fingertips finally touched his palm, he was left feeling lightheaded. Probably because he'd been holding his breath the long seconds it took her to straighten her shoulders and take the necessary step to reach out to him.

Keaton folded his fingers around Brenda's hand, determined never to let her go. Once again, he tugged her to him, and she came. Keaton tucked his wife into his side, where she belonged as they walked out the door and to his rental.

For a strong woman, Brenda was soft. He knew she would never bend easily. That was fine with him.

Keaton had no intention of bending this woman to his will. His goal was to make her melt, to thaw the cold structure she'd erected around her heart. By the flush on her cheeks, he knew his plan was working.

The car ride into town flew by as Keaton continued to hold Brenda's hand in the backseat of the rental. Neither of them talked. At least not with their mouths. He rubbed at her palm while listening to Mac tell some story about their time in Syria.

Brenda rubbed at the space between his knuckles as she stared out the backside window and made noncommittal sounds every so often when Mac paused in his story. Grizz, who was in the driver's seat, kept entirely quiet as he maneuvered the vehicle down the open roads.

Keaton's attention was on the smoothness of Brenda's nails in comparison to the jagged edges of her cuticles. Either she'd broken all ten of her fingernails while out working, or she'd been biting at them from worry. Keaton smoothed his thumb over them again and again as though he could wring out the worry.

The sermon washed over him as well. He sat in the pews beside his wife. Each time they had to rise or bow their heads in prayer, he was obliged to release her hand. He liked it best when they held the Bible between them. Keaton had never been a religious man, but singing hymns and following along the passages, he felt something move him.

After the service, there was a whirlwind of introductions. Keaton would never remember everyone's name. He was so focused on being introduced as Brenda's husband.

"I never thought I'd see the day when Brenda Vance settled down," said one woman, the cloud of her white hair around her heart-shaped face made her look like a pleasant angel. "I thought she was a lesbian."

Keaton blinked. Had he heard that right? He looked up at Brenda, but she was on the other side of the room, encircled by a different bunch of women.

"Now, maybe she'll get in the kitchen and let a man take over that ranch." This was said by a woman with both salt and pepper in her hair. But her lips were pinched as though she'd sucked on a lemon. "Though her cooking skills aren't up to snuff. If you need a home-cooked meal, you come right on over anytime."

Keaton looked from woman to woman. Upon closer inspection, neither of their smiles were genuine. There was a dullness in their eyes, which had only sparked when they'd said disparaging comments about Brenda. "Do either of you actually know my wife?"

The two older women looked at each other. Their shared glance was not one of camaraderie like he and his men would share. There were shields up even as they glanced at each other.

"Brenda is innovating on the ranch, and you're

concerned about what she can do in the kitchen?" he said. "With the profit she's making as an overseer, she can hire a cook."

"I thought the rumor was that they had a marriage of convenience?" the White Cloud said to Salt and Pepper.

"It was," said Keaton. "Until I realized I'd hit the jackpot. I have no intention of letting go of my winnings."

Keaton turned from the two women who clearly had two different faces, none of which were genuine. But before he could get too far, he was confronted with a wrinkled older man who looked as though he'd lived his life hard. Keaton could tell he'd been handsome in his younger days because beside him stood a younger, fresh-faced version.

"It might look like profit, but it'll be short-term," said the older man. His voice was rough, as though there was tobacco growing out of his throat.

"How would you know?" said Keaton.

"Worked on that ranch since before little missy was born. Name's Manuel Bautista. This here is my nephew, Angel."

Keaton wanted to cringe when he shook the elder Bautista's hand. He felt a zap zing into the center of his palm. Not a zing of energy. More like a shock that would've warned him to keep away from the electrical box.

When he took the younger man's hand, he felt a tempered hum. Keaton got the impression that Angel Bautista was an untapped source looking for a path. He wondered if he got the younger man away from the energy suck that was his uncle if he might become a force of nature.

"Your little missus—"

"Brenda," corrected Keaton. "Or Mrs. Keaton."

"Right. She thinks she can run that place by herself. But she's going to need help. Now that a man is there, hopefully, you'll be able to rein her in."

"I'm a military man. We prefer to have a strong woman on our side. Only a weak man would be stupid enough to try and rein a woman in. He'd likely wind up snipped like a steer."

The younger man, Angel, snickered. But he straightened his face when his uncle glared at him. Manuel Bautista turned that hard look back on Keaton.

"We'll see if you're up for the task with Miss Vance —I mean Mrs. Keaton. Or if you'll find yourself outside a broken fence like a wayward bull."

Broken fence? "How did you know the bull got out of the fence?"

Manuel shrugged. His wizened face contorting into something on the border of sinister. "Small town. News travels fast."

Angel looked away. The young man bit at his lip

and wrinkled his nose, as though there was something foul in the air. Keaton thought he smelled it too. His spidey senses were tingling.

"Anyway," said Manuel, "when you're ready to hire an overseer who knows what he's doing, give me a call."

With another grin that made Keaton's gut grumble, Bautista walked off. Angel hesitated. He looked to Keaton. Then he hung his head and followed his uncle.

"We could use the extra hands," said Grizz, coming up behind Keaton.

"Not the old man's," said Keaton.

"Yeah," said Mac coming up to Keaton's other side. "I didn't take to him either. Too bad you didn't get the kid's info. He looked like he'd make a good worker."

CHAPTER EIGHTEEN

For the second time in her life, Brenda slept late. On Monday morning, she rolled over in her bed only a moment before the first rays of the sun stretched up to the horizon. Brenda stretched her arms over her head, letting out a satisfied groan as her muscles and tendons popped.

She should not get used to this. It was completely unprofessional. She'd have to blame it on the previous day's activities. Walking on Keaton's arm. Sitting with her hand in his. Bearing the brunt of the smile and his sparkling gaze and his deep voice filled with compliments for the entire day. The most taxing had been all the concentrating she'd had to do as she shifted into answering to being called Mrs. Keaton.

True, she'd only been called that twice. And both times had been by her brother who was clearly doing it to needle her. It had needled her. Because she'd liked it.

Brenda had always thought that when she got married, she would keep her last name. It was the name of her family ranch. It was a business decision. When anyone said Vance Ranch, she knew they were talking about her. Now, when the name Keaton was uttered, they were, in part, referring to her as well. Was this divided loyalties?

Unlikely. Most of the ranchers and the townsfolk had always eyed her, and her need to modernize, warily. But nearly every person at the church service took an instant liking to Keaton. It had to be the soldier thing. This town was pretty patriotic.

And all the while that Keaton was winning over her lifelong neighbors and friends, he stuck close by her. If he wasn't beside her with his hand at her back, then his gaze was on her. His smile was aimed at her. His attention was somehow focused on her.

So, it was no wonder she'd slept a bit later than usual. It had been a lot to deal with. She was adjusting to a whole new world.

One where she wasn't entirely sure what her place was. She was a touch confused about her role. And she wasn't completely clear about her duties.

For just the briefest of moments, she felt sorry for Manuel Bautista. Was this what he'd felt like when she'd mechanized the things his generation used to do by hand? But no sooner than the first brush of sympathy touched her heart, did Brenda brush it away.

Even if her footing wasn't sure about her new reality, at least she hadn't kicked a gaping hole in the fencing and let out a raging bull. There were boundaries to this marriage. Even though Keaton's hands had been just a bit outside the lines as his fingers had pressed into her back, rubbed warm circles at her palms, brushed a tendril of hair off her forehead and behind her ear.

And don't get her started on his lips. He had only pressed his lips to her temple a few times during the service. When he'd walked her to her room at the end of the night, he'd only kissed her cheek. But by then, Brenda had been wanting to hop a fence.

She settled for hopping out of bed, shoving into her clothes, and headed out in search of the man who was turning her world upside down. When she got to the other side of her door, she knew he was gone.

Her old bedroom door was slightly ajar. In the bathroom, the shower was damp with use. In the kitchen, the coffee mugs were in the sink, and a new pot of coffee was brewing.

She looked out the window, but the soldiers weren't anywhere within view. Her phone buzzed, and she saw a text from Keaton.

Working on the camp. We'll be back in a couple of hours to help with your chores.

Brenda thumbed the message. She decided not to reply. Her hands were needed elsewhere.

The fences on her property were mended. The boundary lines were set. All was in order. But Brenda knew there was always work to be done. She whipped out her to-do list and began checking off morning chores.

By noon, Keaton and the others still weren't back. She could no longer pretend that she wasn't checking for them, that she wasn't waiting for the company. They had their priorities, and she wasn't at the top of their list.

Besides, she didn't need another set of hands to separate the cows from their calves. Climbing atop her horse, she had the mamas and their babies corralled into a paddock behind the barn where she stored the tagging, branding, and castration gear.

Getting the cattle into the entrance was the easy part. Brenda dismounted from her horse, tying the reins to the outside of the fence before closing the gate. Then she moved amongst the cattle.

Cows had a tendency to want to come out the way they went in. That was the plan. Brenda lifted the lower two rungs on the fencing at the entry. Now the entryway had a fork, one leading back out to pasture, the other leading down a small alleyway to a smaller pen. The trick was, only the calves would fit under the rungs of the second entryway.

Brenda stood just off to the side of the entry as the cows began to head out the way they came in. The mama cows kept with the easy and familiar route to Brenda's left. The calves, who were more wary of humans, avoided Brenda and went to the easier route on her right where their bodies neatly fit under the removed rungs of the railing. Proving once more that ranching wasn't about brute force, just a well thought out plan. The whole separation process from getting the cows into the corral to sectioning off calves took less than a half-hour.

"That's a pretty neat trick, boss."

Brenda paused. That wasn't exactly a man's voice. It still held the tenor of youth. Brenda turned to find Angel Bautista. His head was lowered, causing his worn cowboy hat to cast shadows. His lips were pursed as though he tasted contrition.

"What are you doing here, Angel?"

"Your husband sent me to help. He got my number from someone at church and called me this morning." The kid bit at his lip. It took him a long moment before he lifted his head to meet her gaze. "What my uncle did was wrong. And not just the fence. My mama raised me to respect women. She knocked me upside the head when she heard we left you working the ranch on your own."

"Good for her, but I don't want your help."

"I'm sure you don't want it, but I think you need it. And I want to learn. From you."

"You've got your uncle for that."

Angel shook his head. "My uncle is so caught up in a bygone era when it comes to ranches and women. He's on his third wife, you know. The world's changing, that includes how ranches are running. You're one of the few who are trying to adapt. I've only ever wanted to be a rancher."

"What does your uncle think about this?"

"He doesn't know. He's not the boss of me. I'd like that honor to go to you. Even though you're not the easiest person to work for."

"Hey!"

"But I think the best way for me to learn how is here with you. All I need is a chance."

CHAPTER NINETEEN

Keaton sank his hands into the warm earth. The soil here was rich. It moved easily through his fingers as he dug in the trenches. The work was back-breaking, but he could see the rewards he was reaping.

The boundaries of the training camp were finally taking shape. It was all coming together. Not just the camp, but the vision he and his men had had. As well as a vision he hadn't planned on; his wife.

Having Brenda there by his side to see the foundation of his plan coming into view was the only thing that was missing. They'd had to employ the tactic of divide and conquer today. The next few weeks would be hard with all the work they had to do to put their respective plans in motion. For a few days, he'd have to give most of his attention to the camp, but he couldn't wait to get back to the chores on the ranch.

Already, he missed working with the animals, with the Vance Ranch operation, with his life partner who made his heart skip a beat every time he saw her riding toward him on top of a horse. He'd hired one ranch hand to help her out, but he realized he would rather trade spots with Angel Bautista right now and work alongside his wife.

But that wasn't the plan. Brenda had already laid a strong foundation for the ranch. He needed to do the same with the camp.

The sun was setting on this long day. All Keaton wanted was a hot shower, a warm meal, and the feel of his wife in his arms.

Driving across the land, he saw the rest of his life stretched out. He and his brothers would build not only their business but their homes here. His children would grow wild and free, ranging like the cattle. And each night, he'd come home to the most capable woman he knew. And they'd compare checklists.

Grizz and Mac headed inside the big house, where they had each claimed one of the spare rooms on the ground floor. Keaton didn't follow. There was an unsettled air on the ranch. Cows mooed, which was a sound he'd grown used to these last couple of days. But there was a pained note to the chorus of moos. They sounded as though they were in agony.

He walked down a path that led to one of the barns. There were a number of cows out in the pasture. In a smaller pen, were calves. The smaller cattle made sounds that reminded Keaton of a child crying in the night. Standing between the two plots of land was his wife.

Brenda's head was bowed. Her shoulders caved in. Gone was the strong woman he'd met the first time he'd stepped on this land. She looked weary and worn out. Her day had to have been harder than his, especially when she'd only had two sets of hands, and he'd had three. Guilt crashed into him. He should've been there for her.

Keaton wrapped his arms around Brenda from behind. She pulled away from him, jerking out of his hold. When she turned, he saw that there was a branding iron in her hand.

Thank goodness it wasn't hot. But it was aimed at his heart.

Keaton didn't jerk back. He wouldn't mind wearing the Vance brand. It was the letter V with a curlicue at the top like the brim of a cowboy hat. He reached up to the button on his shirt and let it loose.

Brenda watched his action. Her gaze fastened on his bare chest. Could she see his heart pounding on the left side as he waited for her claim?

She lowered the prod and turned back to the

fencing. "Don't sneak up on a woman with a branding iron."

"Don't think I'd mind having your mark on me."

Brenda made a scoffing sound as she shook her head. She set the iron down and began arranging some other items that Keaton couldn't identify. All the while, she kept her back to him.

"Rough day?" he ventured.

One of the calves whined low and long, its large brown gaze fixed on her. Brenda tensed at the sound. She shut her eyes and grimaced.

"What's going on with them?" Keaton asked.

"Separation anxiety. We separated the calves from their sows earlier. In the morning, the calves get branded. Has to be done. By law and because otherwise, anyone could claim them. But as you can hear, they don't like being apart."

"I understand the feeling," Keaton said. "I was away from you all day, and I groaned about it enough that Grizz threatened to throw me in the creek."

Keaton reached for Brenda again. She dodged his advance. She gave him her back as she fussed with some other equipment.

"Bren?" Keaton came to stand in front of her. She kept her head down, not meeting his gaze. "What's going on?"

"I have a lot of work to do."

"Did that Bautista kid not help?"

She met his gaze then. Green eyes flashing the hottest part of a fire. "About that. You have no right to hire help for me."

"I couldn't be here for you. So, I sent help."

It was so slight, but he noticed it. Brenda's lower lip quivered. If she'd let any sound escape, Keaton was sure she'd sound just like one of the forlorn calves. Was she feeling abandoned just like the cows?

"I'm sorry, Bren. But I couldn't be in two places at one time. I'm here now."

"I get it. The camp is your dream. The ranch is mine. We have different priority lists."

"You are my list."

He did reach for her then. The separation was clearly causing them both too much anxiety. She didn't fight his hold. But neither did she accept his words.

"You just met me," she said, crossing her arms over her chest but remaining within his embrace.

"And now I want all of you," he said. "There's something between us. You feel it, too."

Brenda shut her eyes and shook her head, but it was a feeble attempt at denial. "It's not real."

"Feels pretty real to me." He leaned in. Just close enough to touch her lips, but he didn't. He needed her to come to him.

"I feel ..." Her gaze opened. The blazing green had

cooled, but there was still something burning bright. "It's inconvenient. It'll pass."

Keaton let out a harsh laugh, but he did not let her go. He was never letting her go. "You're a hard woman to love, you know that?"

Brenda shook her head. The movement was a tight shake, as though her body didn't believe what she was trying to deny. "You don't love me."

"I'm marching toward it, Brenda. I'm very, very close. And I don't think you're far from me."

She let out a shaky breath. Her fingers, which had been balled into fists under her armpits, crept up to her shoulder blades. She rubbed and squeezed at her forearms. The protective gesture transforming into one of self-comfort.

"You have so many fences up," Keaton continued. "As soon as I get through one, you put up another."

"I'm a cattle rancher," she said. "Fences are my business."

Keaton chuckled as he looked at the obstacle course that was his wife. His heart urged him to bring her closer. But he knew that if he did, she'd put up another fence.

He did it anyway. With his palm at her low back, he pressed their bodies together until a single breath couldn't get between them. He tightened his hold so that she couldn't get away.

"You ever been somewhere and know it's exactly

where you were meant to be?" he asked. "When I saw you, I knew I was meant to be here with you."

Brenda didn't answer. The cows had settled for a few moments. Maybe they'd been calmed by the connection happening just outside the pen.

"I rearranged my master plan for you, Brenda. You're a part of my vision now. I'm bull-headed, like you. I will bust down every fence you put in front of me."

She was soft, pliable now. He felt her will bending. Maybe this would be the last barrier he'd ever have to break through with her.

As if on cue, his phone chimed. Luckily, it wasn't the Vader *Imperial March*, so he didn't feel obligated to answer. But he didn't want another interruption, so he reached in his back pocket for the infernal device.

"Just let me turn this—"

Keaton's words died as he recognized the number. He had to get this call. His hold loosened on Brenda. Like a calf who knew what the new day was going to bring, she slipped out of his hold. Keaton hit TALK on the device. He watched as his wife took one, then another step away from him, gutted that he couldn't immediately follow.

"Yes, sir ...? Yes, construction is going well. We broke ground today and ... You'll be on the ground for a visit tomorrow ...? That's great news. I'll be here to show you around ... Look forward to it."

As Keaton pocketed his phone, the cows took up their wailing moos. The sound kept on late into the night. Keaton barely slept a wink in his wife's childhood bedroom as he worried over how the next day would go.

he cries of the cows kept Brenda up all night. They didn't understand why they were separated from their loved ones. In the morning, they'd get another shock when they were poked in the hind with a hot iron. But that's how life was on a ranch. You couldn't stick around on the land without someone finding their way under your skin.

Brenda had grabbed cold leftovers from the fridge and hid in her room. She stayed corralled in her quarters for the rest of the evening. She didn't dare leave the boundary of those four walls the next morning until she heard Keaton rise, shower, and leave out the front door. And so for another day, she started her day behind schedule.

How had it come to this? She'd made every

provision to protect her assets in that prenup agreement. But, somehow, she'd missed that her heart could get burned in the transaction.

He was close to loving her? That couldn't be possible. He barely knew her.

Except, he did.

He knew the most important thing about her. He knew that she needed help. He knew that more than anything in the world, she craved someone reaching out a hand to her. He'd done that, over and over again. First with his own hand. Then offering the help of his men. And then hiring the help she'd formerly dismissed.

Brenda couldn't deny that Angel had been a great asset to her the other day. And she'd need his help today with the branding and castrating. Those were her two least favorite jobs on this ranch, and it would destroy her to do it on her own today.

But she wouldn't be alone. She saw Angel's truck parked out front. Because her husband had made sure she had the extra hands she needed. Even though the hand Brenda truly wanted was Keaton's.

You ever been somewhere and know it's exactly where you were meant to be?

Brenda had always known she belonged on this ranch. But for the first time since she'd been here on her own, she felt lonely. She was where she was meant to be. But she wasn't with the person she was meant to be with. He'd left the house without even knocking on her door.

And, yes, she'd wanted him to knock on her door. She'd wanted Keaton to remove that large plank of wood that separated the two of them. Because goodness knew that she was incapable of busting out of the tiny pen she'd corralled herself into all on her own. And she was sure that if she kept bucking away from him at every turn, at some point, he would turn to greener pastures.

It was probably already too late. The first rays of sunlight peaked into her window. Down below, the house was quiet. But in the quiet, she smelled strong coffee, buttery eggs, and toasty bread. Just like the animals she tended to, her husband and his friends had left her sustenance to get through her long day in the fields.

With her tail tucked between her legs, Brenda finally dressed and left her bedroom. She paused on the steps when she heard voices in the kitchen. Neither were the honey tons of her husband's voice. Nor were they the deep tones of Grizz. Or the perpetual laughter of Mac. Brenda rounded the corner to find Angel and her brother.

"Walter, what are you doing here?" she asked.

"Your husband said you needed an extra hand

today." Walter piled eggs onto a plate alongside toast. "Why didn't you tell me you didn't have help for the branding? You know I would've come."

Brenda took the plate of food from her brother, taking care to avoid his gaze. At the last second, Walter yanked the plate back.

"Wait a minute," he said, his probing gaze roaming her features. "No, you didn't know that. Did you?"

Brenda shrugged, grabbing the food and going to a seat. "You have your own work. You're living your passion."

"True. But you're my family. I will always make time for you. I make sure you're fed. So, of course, I'm going to make sure you have enough hands to get your work done. Plus, I know branding is your least favorite job here."

Her brother was right. For all her exterior tough act, she hated seeing and hearing the cows cry at the shock of the brand. That's why she'd invested in freeze branding, where liquid nitrogen was used instead of a hot iron. It would still hurt, but research said it would hurt less and was more humane. As humane as burning flesh could be. But it was necessary before she let the calves out to pasture. Otherwise, anyone could claim her cattle as their own.

"I think the three of us can manage," she said after a few bites. "I'm glad Keaton called you. I'm glad Keaton called the both of you."

"That husband of yours is the best hand you've hired, you know," said her brother.

"Yeah, he is. He's helped me more than I can say."

Brenda had spent so much time modernizing and mechanizing so that she wouldn't need all the extra hands. But in the last few days, she'd accomplished more with her husband's hand in the mix. And what had she done? She'd slapped his hand away for helping.

"Bren?" said her brother. "What have you done?"

"Oh, not much," she said, pushing her plate aside. "Just been the pain you know and love."

"Well, that's to be expected."

"Yeah, but will my husband keep putting up with it?" Brenda buried her face in her hands. By the time she scrubbed at her eyes and lifted her head, the two men at the table were looking everywhere but at her. Neither were used to seeing her uncertain. "All right, you two. Enough with the mushy. Let's get to work."

The visible signs of relief were clear on both their faces. Angel was the first to scurry up and toward the back door. Walter fell into step with her and offered her a mug of coffee.

"There's the sister I know."

Stepping out into the cool morning air, Brenda got her wits about her. She and her husband needed to have a long sit-down and discuss the future of their relationship, along with exactly where the boundary lines would be. She was hoping those lines could soon be erased, and they might end up in the same close quarters. But that would have to wait. She had chores to do.

The first thing Brenda became aware of was the quiet near the barns. The mooing had died down, which was unusual. Many ranchers tried to get the separation and branding done within an afternoon. But as she was short-handed, Brenda had opted for an overnight separation.

But coming to the pasture where the mamas were grazing, there was only the normal amount of ruckus. Across the way in the pen was complete silence. The fencing she'd erected was down. The small enclosure was empty.

Last night there had been fifty calves in there. They all were gone. They'd gotten out.

Fifty calves were a year's worth of income. If she didn't recover them, the loss would put her under. But even worse, the calves weren't branded. Meaning anyone could claim that those fifty were their stock.

"This was done by a man," said Angel. "Not an animal."

Angel straightened from the broken fence. Shame colored the young man's cheeks as he looked up at Brenda. They both knew without saying who'd done this.

"We have to stop him," said Brenda. "Where could he have gone?"

"The only way out undetected is the creek."

CHAPTER TWENTY-ONE

"This is a perfect set up for combat training," said the General as they rode up to the training campgrounds.

Keaton looked out at the parcel of land that he was now part-owner of. Grizz and Mac were at his side. Each man standing higher than ten feet tall. The extra height was due to the horses they were each mounted on. General Strauss had suggested they ride out on horseback rather than take a vehicle. As all four of the men knew how to ride, and the horses were available from the Purple Heart Ranch's stables, they all leaped into the saddle at the chance.

With two days of work, Keaton and the guys had sectioned off each of the unique areas for the camp. The materials would be arriving at the end of the week, along with two of the other men. Rusty was still dealing with his family issues.

But, all in all, it was coming together. So, why did Keaton feel like he'd just run the gauntlet, only to look up and see that he wasn't even halfway through? His shoulders ached as though he'd hefted a heavy load across the land. His palms itched with emptiness. His gaze kept tracking back to the creek.

Rivulets of water babbled over rocks. Those paths were already laid before he'd arrived. It took time to make those pathways in the longstanding river. But now the river and the rocks made a harmonious sound as they continued on their way.

Patience and persistence. That's what won any battle. Including, it would appear, a marital relationship.

"So, you'll meet the deadline?"

Keaton blinked, looking up at General Strauss. With just one contract from this man, he and his brothers would be an instant success. But already they had lost three of the ninety days in his plan, and they were about to lose at least three more with the other guys being held up.

He thought of his brothers who'd put their savings into this venture. He recalculated the amount of work that needed to be done. He had planned for hiccups along the way, he always did. It would take twelve-hour days, seven days a week, to make this deadline. That didn't leave any time to give his wife an extra hand on the ranch.

"What am I talking about?" said the General. "Of course, you will. You always bring missions in on time."

"That might not happen this time," said Keaton.

Keaton took a few steps sideways. But with a jerk of the reins, Keaton stopped the behavior. He lifted his head to look back at the three pairs of surprised eyes.

Well, only the General had an arch of surprise in his brows. Grizz closed his eyes, a pained expression creasing his brows. Mac, ever the romantic, did a little fist pump in the air and then pounded his fist once at his heart.

"My wife needs a hand on the ranch," Keaton continued. "She's my family now. And as you know, as Rangers, we never leave anyone behind."

"Didn't realize you'd married," said General Strauss. "So, the rumors about this place are true, then?" He looked around the land, covering the bare fourth finger of his left hand as though a vine from the ground would leap up and trap him.

"Yes," said Keaton and Mac in unison.

"No," said Grizz, but his protest was drowned out by his two friends that believed in the power of love that could set a man on a new and unexpected course.

"Army Rangers turned ranchers? Now I've seen it all." Strauss chuckled as he leaned over his horse, peering off into the distance. "So, there will be cattle runs?"

"Cattle runs?" said Keaton. "No, sir. The ranch and the camp will operate separately. Only my men will work in both places. We wouldn't ask our clients to help on the ranch with our chores."

"Then why are cattle running on your land?" asked the General.

Keaton, Grizz, and Mac had been facing the General in a semi-circle. The three rangers turned their horses around to get a view of what the general was looking at. When he saw the scene, it took Keaton several more seconds to make out what he was seeing.

"Those aren't cattle," said Grizz. "They're calves."

That didn't make any sense. As a rehabilitation facility, the Purple Heart Ranch didn't have many cattle. What cattle they did have were therapeutic, used to help soldiers regain dexterity where appendages were missing by milking cows. And those therapy animals were all in a pasture on the northern side of the ranch. The soldiers here certainly didn't have close to …

Keaton shielded his gaze to get a better view. That had to be about fifty calves running toward them. Toward the creek and away from Vance Ranch. And they weren't alone.

There was a horseman riding behind them. The rider wasn't a she. He was hunched over the horse with what looked like a lasso in his hands. Every other second, he whipped the rope out toward the scurrying calves. The crackle of sound cut the air. It made Keaton's shoulders tense as much as it made the young calves bleed and move their small legs faster.

The sound wasn't what made Keaton's spidey senses tingle. It was the fact that the rider looked familiar to him. The man kept looking over his shoulder like he was running from something.

The man looked back, and his gaze connected with Keaton's. Recognition happened simultaneously in both men's eyes. Keaton felt that hum of dangerous energy, like an electrical box set to explode.

Manuel Bautista rose the whip over his head. He drove his horse, rounding on the cattle, whipping at their feet until they made a turn away from the creek.

"Plans changed," Keaton said as he tightened the reins in his hands. "Looks like we're going on a cattle run, boys."

CHAPTER TWENTY-TWO

Brenda pushed her horse. They couldn't drive a vehicle over this part of the land with its changing terrain. If Angel hadn't guessed where his uncle was headed, she would've wasted time going in the wrong direction and losing precious hours in getting her property back.

The horses made their way across the terrain. Angel was riding at her side. He hadn't wasted time in trying to convince her that he had nothing to do with his uncle's treachery. The young man simply swung into action. That's what proved his innocence and his intentions to Brenda. He stuck by her as they rode on, which told her everything she needed to know.

The creek spilled into the edge of the Purple Heart Ranch territory. Just beyond the creek to the east, the land was all open range. If Manuel was able to cross the creek and reached that pasture, there wouldn't be anything that she could do. Anyone would have the right to claim her cattle and her profit margin.

The only question now was, had Manuel taken the calves through the higher ground just above the creek where the terrain was less forgiving but a quicker path to the open territory? Or had he stuck to the lower ground, which would take him through the creek on an easier stretch of land, but it would also add more time to his getaway.

"He went low," Angel called out as though he could hear her inner thoughts. "Trust me on this."

The two of them maneuvered their horses to take the low road. Brenda let Angel take the lead since he appeared to be the best at tracking. Angel's horse made to step in front of Brenda's, but Angel pulled the reins. There was surprise on his face.

Brenda wondered if it was because she was giving her trust so easily and completely to him? Or if it was because she was stepping aside to allow someone to lead her?

In the past couple of days, she'd learned it wasn't all bad to fall into step beside a man. It definitely wasn't a chore with her husband who had developed a habit of giving her the tiniest of tugs to get her to bend to his will.

"You know, I didn't have anything to do with this," said Angel.

Brenda eyed the kid. He reminded her so much of herself at that age, which wasn't that long ago. When she'd turned eighteen, she'd wanted to break free of authority and do things a new way. But unlike her, Angel was smart enough to listen to both the old ways and the new.

"Yeah," said Brenda. "I know. But you know that when we catch him, I'm pressing charges."

Angel nodded. "I understand. Blood can only go so far."

He was right about that. Walter had stayed behind to call the authorities and get a police report filed. Brenda had hesitated to call Keaton. She knew he was in the middle of sealing the deal with the General, whose contract would fund his operation.

She'd dialed the number because Keaton had said that she was his list. She believed him. She still chose to believe that that was the truth when he didn't pick up. Just because he wasn't there for her at that moment didn't mean that Brenda didn't let herself take that any way other than he was tending to his business. Because that's the kind of man she married.

She knew that if she had reached him, he would've been there, riding by her side. Belatedly, she wondered if her husband knew how to ride? A second later, she saw the answer for herself.

They were nearing the border into the free-range territory. The sounds of pounding hooves came at them from the west. Toward the east, she could make out the calves moving steadily toward the boundary.

Manuel was in their midst. Although it didn't look like he was herding them. It looked like he was trying to outrun them.

Upon second glance, Brenda realized it wasn't the calves her old hand was outrunning. It was the sound of the hooves. Four horsemen rode upon Manuel like they were the Four Horsemen of the Apocalypse. Keaton was in the lead, riding his horse. He was the warrior who had laid claim to her heart, and he was not giving up.

When she reached him, she would tell him that he was the owner of her heart. She'd tell him that she'd happily follow his lead. Heck, she'd wear his brand, meaning she'd take his last name full on. Before this, she'd been planning to hyphenate.

Only it was too late.

She was ready to let her husband take his claim on her. But it looked like she'd need to give up the claim to her calves. Manuel and the calves had reached the border. They were in the free-range territory.

CHAPTER TWENTY-THREE

*K*eaton pushed the horse hard. But the animal didn't seem to mind at all. It had spent much of its time barely running while on the Purple Heart Ranch. It was used as a therapy animal to help wounded soldiers and amputees to heal. But now, it had a real mission.

The four soldiers closed in on the disgruntled, former employee. Keaton was close enough to the elder Bautista to see the whites in his eyes. Though there wasn't much white there to see.

Manuel Bautista's eyes were wide with splotches of red in the corners. He looked the definition of someone who was bloodshot. He was lucky Keaton was unarmed. Though he seriously wanted to pummel the older man with his bare hands.

Bautista dismounted, placing his hands up in the

air. At least he knew when he was caught. But it wasn't Keaton and his men that Bautista had to worry about. Keaton heard the sound of more hooves coming toward them fast. The calves ran past Bautista but quickly began to slow now that there wasn't a whip at their hides. The young cows began to nibble at the bounty beneath their feet.

"Mr. Bautista, you seemed to have misplaced my cattle," said Keaton.

"This is free-range area," said Bautista. "These animals clearly wandered off. They're untagged, so by law—"

"By law?" Keaton swung his leg over and dismounted in one smooth move. "What law? You said this is free territory."

Grizz dismounted with a thunderous shaking of the earth. Followed by Mac, whose friendly smile would give a serial killer chills. And the General who would make any man take a step back.

Bautista swallowed hard as he eyed the crew that cornered him. Around them, the calves feasted happily on the grass, completely unconcerned with the aggression swirling in the air. The older man's eyes looked around wildly, likely for an escape. Keaton saw when a flicker of hope brightened his gaze.

With a glance over his shoulders, Keaton saw Angel Bautista coming toward them on horseback. The young man tipped his hat to Keaton. He barely spared his uncle a glance.

"Angel," said Bautista, "you're my blood. I taught you everything you know."

"What's running through your veins is toxic," said Angel. "And I'm thankful I wasn't paying attention to all your lessons. Otherwise, I'd be about to have my hands behind my back rather than have a future as a ranch hand."

"Well said, kid," said the General. "You ever considered the Armed Forces?"

Angel frowned at the General. Then he made a clicking sound and went about rounding up the cattle. Keaton turned his attention to the rider approaching them.

His wife didn't resemble the avenging angel today. There was a sadness in her gaze as she looked down at Manuel.

"The authorities will be here soon," she said. "Walter called them before we left the ranch. You're going to be held responsible for this, Manuel. As well as kicking down my fence and letting my bull out."

"So, that was him?" said Keaton.

Some of Keaton's anger receded, knowing that Bautista was behind the event that introduced him to his wife. Had that bull not run into his vehicle, he might not have found himself attached to the most amazing woman he'd ever met.

Brenda looked down at him. Her green gaze softened when she met his blue eyes. She reached both arms out to him. Keaton reached up to his wife. Lifting her from her saddle, he brought her body against his. When her feet touched the ground, and she stood on her own, he still did not relinquish his hold.

"You okay?" he asked.

"I'm good. You?"

"Yeah." Keaton brushed a stray strand of hair from her forehead, smoothing the worry lines there as he did so. "Just glad we saw what was happening and were able to go into action."

"Me too," she said, leaning her cheek into the palm of his hand. "We might not have got to him in time."

"I'm going to be there for you," Keaton said.

"I know." Brenda rubbed her cheek against his palm. "You are there for me."

Keaton took a moment to caress the softness of his wife's cheek before clarifying his statement. "I mean, I'm going to loosen the deadline so that I can give you a hand on the ranch."

Brenda blinked up at him. She cupped her hand over his. "But, won't that lose you the contract?"

"No, it won't," said the General. "I know ranch life and cattle runs aren't planned as part of the training, but if it's possible for that to change, I think we can work something out about the deadline."

"What are you saying?" asked Keaton.

"This is a need that's not being met," said the General. "Most of the time, my men are in places where we have to use pack animals or are working with farmers and herders. I don't know any other training camp that has this feature."

"It's not a feat—" Before Grizz could complete his sentence, Mac jabbed him in the chest.

"We weren't sure if it was a viable addition," said Mac. "But now that we see you're on board, I'm sure we can work something out."

"I love it," said the General. "Army Ranger training on a ranch. It's genius. Plan an actual cattle run, and I'll be back for that myself."

"You know," said Mac, "we were thinking about adding that to the curriculum ..."

The voices of the two men trailed off as they headed back to their mounts. Grizz dismounted and grabbed Manuel Bautista, dragging him bodily after the other two. Angel had most of the calves in hand and was leading them back the way they came.

That just left Brenda and Keaton, still wrapped up in each other's embrace. Keaton splayed his hand over his wife's low back, reveling in the warmth of her. Brenda leaned her forehead against his chest, then rolled her head until her ear rested against his heart.

"So, we're not fighting anymore?" Keaton asked as he tucked his wife's head under his chin.

"No," she sighed. "I'm not fighting it anymore. You're just too bull-headed."

Keaton chuckled. He nudged the top of Brenda's head with his nose until she tilted her head back. Then he stole her lips in a kiss that left no room for arguments.

"Thank you for rearranging your plans for me," Brenda said when Keaton let her up for air. "Now, how about we go home and make some plans together?"

A low rumble sounded at the back of Keaton's throat. "That has to be the sexiest thing anyone has ever said to me."

"Oh, yeah?" she said. "Just wait until you see the spreadsheets I have planned for us."

Keaton held out his hand. Brenda placed her hand in his. Their palms pressed together. Then their fingers entwined. From this day forward, they would plan together, set achievable goals, and check off lists in the masterplan of their lives. Unlike all of the other plans he crafted, for this one, there would be no Plan B.

EPILOGUE

Grizz was glad the day was over. The authorities had come and arrested Manuel Bautista. The General had signed the contract on the dotted line. All was right with the world again.

As he watched Bautista being carted away, he had sympathy for the guy. Grizz knew what it was like to reach higher than his station. To want something he had no right to. But unlike the old man, Grizz would never take what was not his.

The powers that be thought he had. His superiors thought he'd broken rules and overstepped his bounds. He hadn't. But he had stayed silent as something had gone down. So he was tarnished by proximity.

That was pretty much the story of his life. Even

joining the elite Army Ranger force had not shaken the stank of his lower class breeding from his back. The stank wasn't the only thing from his past that was clinging to him. The poverty was back.

The monies owed him by the army were being tied up while his case was under review. Grizz hadn't expected it to take so long. The others had all put in their share to fund the camp. Keaton hadn't pressed his oldest friend. But now that they were on the land, bills were coming due.

Grizz knew Keaton would front him the money. His best friend always had since they were kids. But Grizz hated handouts. He always insisted on earning his own way.

Being an equal member and investor in this venture was his dream. But that dream was turning into a nightmare while he waited for his judgement.

The Sheriff's car disappeared down the road. Bautista had made a bad decision late in life. Bad decisions always planted themselves in frizz's way. They were like land mines he could never see until he was right up on it.

"Hey, Grizzly Bear."

The voice came from behind him. He had learned not to have his back to the enemy. She wasn't the enemy. But she was the greatest danger to him.

Grizz turned to find a young woman standing behind

him. All five foot four inches and one-hundred-ten pounds of her. Bright blue eyes filled with intelligence and mischief -a lethal combination. Flaming red hair that rivaled a blaze, a warning not to touch. As if he needed a warning to keep his hands off his best friend's sister.

"What are you doing here, Patty Cakes?" he said.

Grizz had known Patricia Keaton since she was a baby. She's been attached to his leg after her first step. He'd thrilled at being her protector. Coming from the home he came from, he loved the idea of being a hero. And Patty hero worshiped him. Until the day she decided she wanted to be his heroine.

"I came to meet my new sister-in-law and see my two favorite guys," she said. "Don't I get a hug?"

A hug was dangerous. A hug meant that she'd be in his arm. She wasn't all gangly limbs anymore. Patty had curves now. Those curves were headed straight for him.

Grizz took a step back, but it was too late. She was on him. She wrapped her arms around his neck like she would put him in a submission hold. Because he could never say no to her. Except the day when she had asked him to give her her first kiss. He'd told her no. But inside Grizz had felt a growl rise from his gut into his throat.

Mine, that primal beast wanted to shout.

Mine, it wanted to howl now that the woman who

fit him perfectly was back in his arms where she belonged.

Grizz ducked away from Patty's hold. In the distance, he saw Keaton headed for them. With his background, he knew he wasn't the guy for a girl like Patty. And with the uncertainty of his future, he knew he would never be.

Grizz may be thinking it's not meant to happen between him and Patty.
But Patty has a very different plan.
Watch how these two wind up in a marriage of convenience when
"The Rancher takes his Best Friend's Sister."

Order your copy today!

Shanae Johnson was raised by Saturday Morning cartoons and After School Specials. She still doesn't understand why there isn't a life lesson that ties the issues of the day together just before bedtime. While she's still waiting for the meaning of it all, she writes stories to try and figure it all out. Her books are wholesome and sweet, but her are heroes are hot and heroines are full of sass!

And by the way, the E elongates the A. So it's pronounced Shan-aaaaaaaa. Perfect for a hero to call out across the moors, or up to a balcony, or to blare outside her window on a boombox. If you hear him calling her name, please send him her way!

You can sign up for Shanae's Reader Group at http://bit.ly/ShanaeJohnsonReaders

Also By Shanae Johnson

The Rangers of Purple Heart

The Rancher takes his Convenient Bride

The Rancher takes his Best Friend's Sister

The Rancher takes his Runaway Bride

The Rancher takes his Star Crossed Love

The Rancher takes his Love at First Sight

The Rancher takes his Last Chance at Love

The Brides of Purple Heart

On His Bended Knee

Hand Over His Heart

Offering His Arm

His Permanent Scar

Having His Back

In Over His Head

Always On His Mind

Every Step He Takes

In His Good Hands

Light Up His Life

Strength to Stand

The Rebel Royals series

The King and the Kindergarten Teacher

The Prince and the Pie Maker

The Duke and the DJ

The Marquis and the Magician's Assistant

The Princess and the Principal